NV 6/85

D1152948

11 MAR 2000

SKELMERSDALE

FICTION RESERVE STOCK LL 60

AUTHOR BURNFORD, S.	CLASS F
TITLE Bel Ria: dog of war.	No. 57709058

LANCASHIRE COUNTY COUNCIL

This book should be returned on or before the latest date
shown above to the library from which it was borrowed

LIBRARY HEADQUARTERS, 143 CORPORATION STREET, PRESTON, PR1 8RH

a30118 043039910b

BEL RIA

Also by Sheila Burnford

THE INCREDIBLE JOURNEY
FIELDS OF NOON
WITHOUT RESERVE
ONE WOMAN'S ARCTIC
MR NOAH AND THE SECOND FLOOD

BEL RIA

Dog of War

Sheila Burnford

LONDON
MICHAEL JOSEPH

First published in Great Britain by Michael Joseph Ltd
52 Bedford Square, London WC1B 3EF
1977

© 1977 by Sheila Burnford

All Rights Reserved. No part of this publication
may be reproduced, stored in a retrieval system,
or transmitted in any form or by any means,
electronic, mechanical, photocopying, recording
or otherwise, without the prior permission
of the Copyright owner

ISBN 0 7181 1634 8

Set and printed in Great Britain by
Tonbridge Printers Ltd, Peach Hall Works, Tonbridge, Kent
in Plantin eleven on thirteen point on paper supplied by
P. F. Bingham Ltd, and bound by
Dorstel Press, Harlow

57709058
NA ·

In Memoriam
1939–1945

The author makes grateful acknowledgement to the following: The Canada Council of Arts, the Imperial War Museum, the B.B.C. Written Archives, and Ministry of Defence (Navy Department).

'Let Hercules himself do what he may,
The cat will mew and dog will have his day.'

Hamlet V I (313)

Part One

I

Its flaking red paint almost obscured by dust, an old swayback grey horse between the shafts, the caravan stood out even among the bizarre lines of transport that filled the last free roads of France that bright June morning in 1940. Alone it creaked along against the civilian refugee traffic, the endless frieze of handcarts and ancient perambulators, wheelbarrows and farmcarts, the weary disillusioned people. All were on the open road, but only the caravan belonged by custom to the open road, only those who lived and had their world by it were true vagrants. It was this outlandish rightfulness that turned the caravan into an affront to the fleeing homeless. Only a few short weeks ago such passers-by would have stirred interest, curiosity, and even sometimes envy of a here today and gone tomorrow existence, but today there was only a sullen resentment and distrust of strangers who took a road leading back toward the approaching enemy.

Even the little dog that led the caravan was different. There were other dogs on the road that day, but taking their mood from their owners they padded along as dispiritedly as the heels that moved before them, tails low, panting, grey and formless as the dust. This alien dog that alone passed the other way took vivid form: head and tail held high, trotting along with important cheerful intent, sometimes almost prancing, at a carefully kept distance ahead. It appeared to lead the horse, for the reins lay slack in the hands of an ancient man huddled in layers of shawls on the wide seat. A tiny monkey, perched on his shoulder, gazed intently ahead as though making up for his lack of interest.

Walking at the side by the ditch, a tall black-clad granite-faced woman led a shuffling, shabby bear, which occasionally sank back on its hindquarters with muzzled head swinging low, and refused to move. Each time, after a brief glance back, but apparently unsummoned, the dog halted the horse by sitting down before it, then ran back to bark encouragement while the woman alternately tugged on the chain and prodded the brown bulk with her foot. When the bear was once more on the move, the dog returned to rouse the horse and the wheels creaked into action again. A young donkey on a rope halter tied to the back of the caravan completed the procession.

Hard-pressed by the German spearheads thrusting to close the gap between them and the last escape route in France, there was still an intermittent stream of military traffic and troops passing on the opposite side of the road, heading for St Nazaire on the Britanny coast. The remnants of Operation Panther and the weary stragglers from the general retreat across France after Dunkirk threaded through the painfully slow civilian congestion with frequent hold-ups while broken-down vehicles were manhandled out of the way. On the northbound side, only a rare rearguard squadron of light tanks, armoured cars, or the occasional army truck being driven back to the wrecking dump pulled out to pass the caravan, so that almost always it was the civilian traffic opposite that had to give way or take to the ditches, and this sometimes engendered outright hostility.

The woman and the old man appeared either deaf or totally indifferent to the verbal abuse from across the road; at each enforced halt they and their animals seemed to freeze into stony immobility, waiting only for some signal to re-activate them. But whether this was communicated by the woman or by the leader, the dusty little dog, who sat back squarely on his haunches as though propped there by rigid front legs, it was impossible to tell. Certainly there was no movement to the reins from the bundle on the seat, into whose folds of shawls the monkey would disappear during the halts.

Corporal Sinclair of the Royal Army Service Corps who, by one of the more lunatic entanglements of red tape and chaotic communication, had orders to drive his empty truck back from the coast to be wrecked at Montoire, had inched along at the heels of the donkey for a long mile, unable to swing out and pass, his vision ahead almost obscured by the high, swaying caravan. He had followed it so slowly and so closely that he felt almost as though he were part of it.

Once, returning to the truck after manoeuvring a broken-down hearse off the road, he had tried to make communication, smiling at the woman as he bent to pat the dog, but the head beneath his fingers was directed only to the woman, and her dark face was unresponsive. A distant stare rewarded his sketchy French. He tried again, proffering a packet of cigarettes. After a moment's hesitation she took one, and tucked it behind her ear, refusing another; but for a fleeting moment Sinclair saw a relaxation in the grimly set lips and, as though taking his line from her, the dog stirred his short tail. Soon after that the road cleared and the caravan and truck started off again.

After half a mile, however, they met a straggling platoon of Pioneers who had missed their rendezvous somewhere. The sergeant stopped the truck and suggested that the soldier do a kindly about-turn and carry his flagging grandfathers back down the road until they found some other available transport. Sinclair had time in hand. His orders were to report first to Movement Control at Savenay when and however was possible. The useful life of this vehicle might as well be extended. The Pioneers piled gratefully in with their picks and shovels and he set off.

It was noon before he caught up with the caravan on his return trip, during a long halt while a convoy passed at erratically-spaced intervals. It was hot, dusty and noisy, the sun beating down from a cloudless sky. The woman had taken out a goatskin water carrier which she handed up to the old man. He threw back his head and directed a stream of water into his mouth, then in turn she drank. The tethered bear sank down on its haunches, the extended forepaws pressed together, begging. She filled a bottle; clasping it like a child, the bear inserted the open end through the steel and leather of the muzzle and tilted the contents down its throat. A canvas bucket was set in turn before the horse and donkey. Finally she filled an enamel bowl, and the dog came running to lap.

A panting black mongrel crossed the road, thrust its head into the bowl and gulped avidly. The little dog moved aside, unaggressive, until the woman intervened and edged off the intruder. A young woman with a child on her hip crossed the road and held up a tin pitcher, asking for water. There was no reply, and she resorted to sign language, pointing at the child, the pitcher, her mouth. Finally she shouted, so loudly and angrily that the child howled. Without any recognition the dark woman continued to hold the bowl while her dog lapped. Only when the other spat contemptuously, directly into the bowl, did she straighten up and, with eyes blazing, she hurled it at the young woman's skirts. Quick as a flash, although encumbered with child and pitcher, the mother picked up the bowl and aimed at the little dog, who leaped for the shelter of the driving seat. A stone flew across the road from the hand of an ancient but suddenly agile crone, and found a target on the bear's nose; as it whimpered and shook its head, droplets of bright blood scattered over the dust. Another stone followed to rattle on the caravan, and another.

Sinclair got out, prepared to do he knew not what, but bound by some obscure north versus southbound loyalty, and outraged by the pitiful senselessness of this shabby bear pawing feebly at its bleeding nose.

14

He was saved from action by the last tank rumbling by to meet the last carrier of the convoy; they met in the middle of the road, and chaos intervened. When the road was cleared, he returned to find the caravan lurched precariously in the ditch, the dog barking by the plunging straining horse while the woman alternately pushed and hung on to the tilting side. Even the old man had been galvanised into enough life to flap the reins. The sullen audience across the road, once more on the move, trudged by indifferently. With the aid of a passing despatch rider and an inexplicably bicycling Sikh rifleman, the soldier got the caravan back on the road. At the last heave, the back near wheel collapsed, the axle pin sheared. Despite the tilted axle shaft, the caravan miraculously remained upright. The woman suddenly looked drawn and exhausted, close to despair. Sinclair produced a wheel jack.

'All in the day's work,' he said cheerfully, and showed her how to use the jack. 'You might as well keep it,' he added later, when the wheel was replaced, and a spare pin fitted. But despite eloquent pointings from the jack, to himself, and then to her, she still looked dubiously at him. At last she rummaged in her skirt pocket to produce a small purse from which she extracted a few coins. The soldier closed her fingers around the money, then shook the hand with a smile of refusal. He pointed to the water carrier and indicated that he would rather have a drink, but she upended the skin, with a somewhat wry smile at its emptiness.

They were standing by the driving seat, their heads on a level with the dog sitting there, his bright, alert eyes under a top-knot of pulled-back hair, going from one face to the other, as though interpreting every expression. The doll-sized head of the monkey, now perched on his back, peered ludicrously over the top-knot.

The woman's face suddenly cleared as she looked at them. She clicked her fingers. The monkey immediately transferred to her shoulder, the dog jumped down and rose to his hindlegs beside her. With the occasional slight motion of her hands, she put him through a small repertoire of tricks. Importantly, accompanied by the faint sweet tinkling of a bell around his neck, he strutted back and forth, turned three rapid backward somersaults, then finally sat up at their feet with one paw raised in salute. The woman gazed down at him, her face softened by obvious pride. The dog looked back at her with beaming eyes, his slight body quivering as she reached in her pocket and tossed him some small titbit which he caught in mid-air.

The soldier applauded. Clearly this display had been his reward. He turned to go. The monkey in her arms pouted its lips, then smacked them in an astonishingly loud kissing noise, and held out an upturned pink paw. The soldier laughed and shook it. 'Goodbye,' he said 'And good luck – *bonne chance, madame.*' But already she was hurrying to untie the bear tethered to a steel stake in the shade of the overgrown hedge.

She tugged and prodded and shouted, but the bear lay unmoving, its muzzle half-buried in leaves, the little eyes sunken and apathetic. She broke off a branch as a switch and raised it threateningly. The bear whimpered, closed its eyes and winced in anticipation, and at this she gave up the struggle. She threw away the branch, then, hands on hips, stared down, indecisive. Just as Sinclair was about to drive off she ran towards him, and pointed to his rifle. Somehow she made him understand; there was no food for the bear, it was only an added burden, it had been someone else's livelihood, this dancing bear, never theirs . . .

Sinclair did not hesitate; to his mind, this sorry beast would be better out of its misery. He slipped a round in his rifle and followed her back. She held the bear's chain, with no change of expression on her set face, and it was all over in a second. Thriftily she removed the muzzle, collar and stake, and the soldier pulled some branches over. She took his hand and shook it warmly, then pointed from the mound at their feet to

16

the old man at the reins. For an astounded moment, the soldier thought that he was being asked to dispose of him too. But it must have been merely a comment on how much easier life would now be for, with a smile of satisfaction, she swung herself up beside the ancient bundle and took the reins herself. The monkey, chattering excitedly, jumped on to her lap. The dog had already taken up his station ahead of the horse. She accorded the soldier a brief nod as he drove past.

The retreating traffic petered out markedly as Sinclair drove on. The caravan had given him a brief refreshing interlude from being one with this humiliation of retreat, this frustrating absurdity of driving these miles solely to destroy his vehicle, then to become himself one with this desperate flight from France. At least the caravan and its quaint entourage had a complete objectivity in the midst of this grey uncertainty – an uncertainty that was exemplified when he reached Savenay, only to be ordered by a chaotic Movement Control to drive the truck back again to Montoire, and there to hand it over to the wrecking crew. After that, he was to make his way back to St Nazaire for embarkation. 'Get there after dusk,' the sergeant advised. 'It's not a healthy place in daylight.'

Sinclair was one of the last drivers to leave the blazing dump at Montoire, and it was there at the very moment of departure, ironically, after weeks of bombing and shellfire during the long haul back across France from the over-run Dunkirk beaches, that he was wounded; a tin exploded from a burning NAAFI truck and tore a jagged path across his ribs, so that every breath he took now was a searing reminder. Someone had covered the wound with a field dressing.

There was only one truck left at the dump for the eventual transportation of the wrecking crew itself, and as he could no longer help he left to take his chances of a lift on the road. By now the situation was totally confused, he was told, and all communication had broken down. France was almost over-run, but here and there, apparently, between the advancing spearheads of the German columns, were clear lanes down which a man might yet make his way to the coast.

He shouldered his rifle and pack and started off down a deserted side road. An atmosphere that was almost calm lay over the land now, of resignation perhaps; those who remained went about their business, hoarding, burying, destroying, preparing for the long siege ahead. For some it was but a repetition of another time, another occupation, the years of familiar endurance to be faced once more. In the end, the day of freedom must surely break; in the meantime children must be comforted to sleep, old people's querulous needs be met; there were eggs to be gathered and cows to be milked.

The road stretched out before the soldier, a composite of all the pictures he had ever seen of roads left in the wake of a retreating army in other countries, other wars, something he had never expected to see himself; the abandoned wrecked equipment of an army haphazard with civilian pathos, the stiff-legged carcass of a horse, a handcart with a broken axle, an ancient Citroen on its side, one wheel turning in the soft wind, a battered doll face down in a patch of oil beside it. Half in, half out of a ruined basket, a carrier pigeon with one wing shot away crouched, life still in the glazed uncomprehending eye. The soldier turned back after five paces and broke its neck, watched only by the yellow satanic eyes of two goats grazing down the hedge. In the field beyond, a small herd of thin cows, bellowing with the pain of unmilked udders, pressed against a gate leading to the farmyard, but the only sign of life in the farmhouse was a cat sitting on the window ledge. Clear above the bellowing, a thrush sang jubilantly from an ivy-covered oak; a short song, and when it was finished there was a moment of listening silence when even the cows were silent, and then the distant rumble of guns from the coast intruded. The soldier shifted the weight of pack and rifle and plodded on down the macabre desertion of the road.

He was very, very tired. He could not remember when he had last slept for more than a snatched hour at a Rest Centre;

he had lost a good deal of blood, and he now felt as dazed and numb with hurt as the pigeon, as uncomprehending as the cows. He tried to take his mind off his body, to think of other things as he walked: of his young wife, now working in a munitions factory; of his father, in the long west highland glen leading from the sea loch. It had been winter when he was last there, the red stags awaiting his coming with feed on the white windswept hills. Now the hills would be tender green, sunlit and shadowed by cumulus, the stags ranging far beyond the glen, the hinds high and secret with their new born calves. His father would be doing the work of two men, a solitary old man in the white cottage that had been home . . .

He tried to measure his walk now in terms of landmarks on the lonely road that snaked around the loch shore from the cottage to, say, Balluchmore village . . . Two miles on and he would cross the humpbacked bridge soon, just around that corner . . . three miles and it would be the stand of mountain ash above the bothy. Sick and giddy he stood at the side of the road, looking in vain for the ruined keep that should be coming into view now on its narrow peninsular, Beinn Bhreac should be there, looming up behind . . . The soldier's knees gave way, and he folded gently into the shallow ditch.

2

Sinclair came to, and with no sense of alarm found himself looking directly into a pair of eyes only a few inches away. They were merry, interested eyes, and he recognised them at once, one partly obscured by a few wisps of hair escaped from a familiar top-knot. As the dog's head bent closer, the muzzle touched his temple briefly, and he heard a faint tinkling. His eyes travelled peacefully up, and he saw a pair of feet in worn espadrilles, thick black stockings, and the hem of a dusty black skirt. He felt no surprise; it was almost as though he had expected her.

He raised his head and shoulders and looked around, wincing involuntarily at the stab of pain. The wagon was drawn up on the verge of the road, the familar huddle in front, the weary head-low horse and donkey. He tried to get to his feet but the world went into a sickening spin. The woman helped him, speaking with an incomprehensible urgency as she pointed down the road. She slung the rifle over her shoulder, then with an arm like steel around his shoulders, she drew him out of the ditch and through the open door of the caravan.

Now he heard the noise of approaching engines, and understood her haste as she bundled him inside, pushing him out of the way on to a narrow bunk that ran down the length of one side at the same time as she scooped bundles of sacks, blankets and quilts off an elaborate brass bedstead opposite. She thrust the rifle under the sagging mattress, then turned to the soldier and, almost before he knew it, he was stretched out and under the covers, the bundles replaced on top. She indicated a tiny sliding ventilation grille in the side, sliding it fractionally open before dropping a musty pillow over his head and pulling up the covers. Something – a bundle of withys, he guessed – was thrown across his feet, then finally he felt the light living weight of the dog as it stretched across his thighs. She spoke one soft single word, then the door slammed. Seconds later the caravan creaked and swayed into movement. The soldier gave himself up for the moment to the musty darkness, the steady soothing clop-clop of hooves, and drifted away again.

An awareness of alteration in the light warmth across his thighs roused him; the weight was no longer relaxed, and he heard the accompanying tinkle of an alerted head. The caravan halted, and now there were men's voices, harsh and commanding, the revving of engines, someone shouting. Although he knew not a word of German, it was not difficult to interpret what was going on outside. The caravan must have reached one of the forward posts of the German thrusts, and its whys and wherefores were being challenged.

He heard the woman's voice, apparently arguing, but not understood by her interrogators, and the sound of heavy boots approaching. As the wagon springs creaked to a new weight and the door was flung open, he lay rigid, his breath held. He felt the dog sit up, the quick movement of his tail, and heard the woman's voice again. Then, extraordinarily, the sound of laughter. The dog jumped down, the boots and voices moved off to the side, and someone, perhaps the old man, closed the door behind his head. The woman's voice rose again, loud and audacious now, and once more the mystifying laughter.

He turned cautiously to the tiny strip of light under the covers from the ventilation grille. He put his eye to this peephole. The effect was dramatic, like looking down on a small spotlit stage, for in his circumscribed view he could see only a semi-circle of boots and the grey-green of German uniform tucked into them. In the centre of this stage, now adorned with a small cluster of bells secured to the top-knot and tinkling circlets on each forepaw, was the little dog. Only a few inches away from his eyes were the black skirts and dusty espadrilles of the woman, the toe of one of them raised even as he heard three short, sweet, flute-like notes close to his head. Evidently the old man was providing the music.

On the fourth note the toe began to tap, and the dog rose to his hindlegs and began to dance. The tune had a lilting rhythm, and in perfect time he pirouetted in a circle, forepaws held out and head held high. The music changed in tempo, slower now, and at the end of each phrase the dog nodded his head so that the silvery bells accompanied each last three notes of the repeated phrase. Now he brought the forepaws into action, one at a time, each cluster of bells set in a different pitch to the nodding head.

It was the performance of a virtuoso. The strangest thing was that there seemed nothing preposterous, only an inherent grace and precision. The little dog danced as though he lived for it, as though he would will his audience to listen to his bells and live for it too.

Not far away, guns rumbled a reminder. Three-quarters of the western world lay reeling in the bonds of occupation, the wake of smouldering destruction left by these grey-green uniforms. A few short miles would soon end the agony of France, and then all Europe would be over-run – yet for this moment, in this one place, there was nothing but a silvery tinkling and a lilting tune and an audience who had become children again, spellbound before a dog who danced on a sunlit road to the bidding of the flute.

So enchanted had Sinclair been too, that he felt almost a momentary irritation when the skirt moved and the palm of a hand occasionally lowered and raised obscuring his view, bringing the reality that these concealed signals probably coincided with the movements of head and paws. Yet the dog never appeared to look anywhere but directly ahead. The flute quickened in tempo and the little dancer spun in a small tight circle, the bells sounding wildly; and then, like a clock-work toy running down, slower and slower, the dog sank down to his haunches, shaking the bells on each extended fore-paw in turn; then the paws lowered to the dust, the body following, until, finally, the last shake of bells to the final note of the flute, the head drooped and the dog lay still.

There was a momentary hush, as of an audience bringing itself back to reality, then a ragged round of applause and voices again. The woman spoke one soft sibilant, the ears flickered briefly, then the dog leaped into life to make a suddenly comic bow to the semi-circle of boots. The fingers clicked and he came running, with open mouth and lolling tongue, so that he appeared to be laughing. The fingers removed the bells from the paws, then slipped into a side pocket to return with some small reward of food. Two arms now made a circle and the dog jumped through it and out of Sinclair's sight.

For a brief second he saw the doll-like figure of the monkey scuttle into view holding a tin cup, then the black skirts curtained off his view altogether. Clear above the guffaws of laughter and voices, the woman's voice rose in a new note, almost harsh and demanding, so that the soldier was re-minded of a huckster at a fair. He heard more laughter, then a tinny rattle of coins, and the brazen comments of the woman. The show was over, and as though to affirm this there was a burst of mortar fire from comparatively close range and shouted orders followed by a crescendo of revving engines.

The encounter must have taken place at a crossroads, for when the caravan started up again Sinclair felt it swaying to a right-angled turn, and the road surface was rougher. At least they were not travelling away from the coast now. He must get out as soon as possible; he could cut down lanes, across fields, and rejoin the road. He lay still, fighting the urge to sleep, until he reckoned that they must have covered a reasonable distance. Then summoning every ounce of will power, he struggled up, pushed aside the covers, and retrieved his rifle from under the mattress. The cold steel was a sobering reminder.

He tapped on the half door. It opened a crack and he peered through, looking ahead to an empty potholed road. The craggy profile of the woman turned to look back along the road. She gave a grunt of apparent satisfaction, but when Sinclair pushed the door wider, intending to jump, she pressed it back and spoke in an unexpectedly sweet clear voice, quite different from the harsh fairground tones he had last heard. Words that were as incomprehensible as ever, but their message was clearly stressed; he must get under cover again. To his insistent repetition of 'St Nazaire, *St Nazaire* ...' as he touched the rifle and pointed to himself, she merely nodded calmly, pointed to the sun and shook her head. Then, as though to reassure him, she cracked the whip competently above the horse's ears, and with a further slap of the reins she increased the pace.

Presently they turned off the road and creaked to a halt. The woman came through and the soldier removed his covers with relief. She opened a shutter and a shaft of sunlight fell on a bright red stain on his blouse. The dog jumped on the bed and sniffed at it with interest, tail wagging fast, until the woman pushed him gently aside and undid the buttons, her face concerned. The field dressing was soaked through. She replaced it with what looked like a wad of moss, smearing it first with some aromatic salve out of a rusty tin, then bound it firmly with a strip torn off the hem of her underskirt. The net effect was extraordinarily soothing and comfortable.

They were halted on a sandy track under a clump of pines. In an almost leisurely fashion the woman began to unharness the horse, then, when the shafts were down, she helped the old man out, reached up for a folding stool and seated him close to the wheel. He was still holding his flute; she took it from him, stuck it in his pocket and substituted a clay

24

pipe which the monkey promptly removed to its own mouth, scampering up on to the dog's back out of reach. The old man reviled them both with furious impotent grunts. Next she lit a small pressure stove which was soon hissing beneath a blackened billy can. Sinclair could barely restrain his impatience until he realised that whatever she was doing she was wary as a poacher, eyes and ears alertly sweeping the countryside.

Lastly, accompanied by the dog with his proportionate little jockey hanging around his neck, she walked quickly to the top of the rise and surveyed the land from there. The dog's head turned in precisely the same arc as hers. Satisfied, she turned back and brewed bitter, strong tea, lacing Sinclair's mug from a small medicine bottle rummaged out of the old man's pocket.

The concoction flowed through Sinclair's veins in a glorious heartening molten fire. As he sipped, she took a twig and made a sketch map on the sandy ground; here was the road where they had picked him up, the crossroads where they had turned east; and here was a back road, too meandering and narrow for military traffic, that eventually met up with a secondary road leading into St Nazaire. He must set off cross-country for the first part. He followed her pointing finger to the south where high up in the pale still sky puffs of gun-smoke expanded like parachutes. His arm rested on the donkey's back, his fingers absently tracing the cross there, the coarse, sunwarmed hair suddenly nostalgically familiar and normal, real in this unreal world.

The woman's voice broke in: '*Mort pour la Patrie!*' she said with command. Sinclair looked up, startled at this inexplicable announcement, delivered with such obvious utter contempt, and for the first time in a recognisable language. The dog interpreted by rolling over and over on the sketch map, scattering the sand, then lying still, as though dead. Then, to a mocking '*Vive la France!*', the small corpse sat up with a ludicrous imitation of a salute. The voice was at total variance with the almost doting expression on the dark face, an expression reflected in the intense concentration of the eyes below, the slight compact body tensed like a coiled spring in anticipation. She pointed, and in a single bound the dog jumped up on to the donkey's back. She felt in her pocket, found nothing there, and laid her hand on his head in reward instead, gently rubbing behind one ear.

It was time to go. Unable to express his gratitude in words to this enigmatic, indomitable woman who had taken such a risk for him, Sinclair unconsciously did the one right thing and spoke the one universally accepted word. 'Bravo!' he said simply, and he too patted the dog's head, an action acknowledged by the stumpy tail and the sensual almost cat-like inclination of the head towards his fingers. He felt in his pocket for the remains of a biscuit. It was taken gently and fastidiously, then laid on the donkey's back until the release of a smiling nod of assent from the woman.

The old man suddenly made a grunting imperative noise, holding out the medicine bottle. Only when he saw his offering stowed in the soldier's pocket did he sink again within his shawls – like a tortoise retracting into its shell, he seemed to Sinclair as he said goodbye and set off up the sandy track.

On the crest of the rise he looked back. The woman had already excluded him, her back turned as she fed the horse. Only the dog, and the monkey once more astride his back, watched his departure with grave interest.

3

The soldier covered the ground in the easy strides of a hillman. He felt surprisingly refreshed and alert, the pain warmly contained under the comfort of the moss dressing. He had no wish for transportation now even if it had magically appeared. It could not be much more than ten miles to the coast and, remembering the sergeant at the dump's warning, he reckoned on reaching the docks after nightfall.

He skirted the last field and as he emerged on to the narrow lane described by the woman, he heard the all too familiar engines of a Stuka, and almost immediately saw it sweep across the fields towards him, well below tree top level. Even as he flung himself down in the ditch with a gasp of sudden appalling pain in his ribs, he wondered why, for there had been nothing in the fields but a distant scattering of cattle and himself. The Stuka screamed over, its machine gun raising spurts of earth, pinging on the tin roof of a cattle shelter, and then banked sharply to roar back over the fields, gun still blazing.

'Bloody lunatic,' shouted Sinclair indignantly after it, and started off again, keeping a weather eye open for its predictable return.

Presently, he was very slowly overtaken by his first military traffic – an RAOC sergeant pedalling along on an ancient bicycle with hard rubber tyres. A slight young Lancashire Fusilier with grotesquely swollen feet, his boots slung around his neck, sat sideways on the cross bar. A black collie panted along behind. 'Sorry, mate, full up,' said the sergeant as he wobbled past.

Sinclair stepped out beside them for a few yards. 'Watch out for a Daredevil of the Skies in a Stuka,' he said. 'The type that would shoot up a turnip field for the hell of it—'

'*Him*—' said the sergeant, disgust flooding his face. 'He conquered a couple of gypsies and a wagon back there. . . .'

'In a clump of pines – an old man and a woman?'

'I wouldn't know, but there were two bodies all right,' said the sergeant. 'The wagon was blazing—'

'They had animals?' asked Sinclair.

'I shot a horse,' said the sergeant briefly, 'and there was a donkey, but I missed it – it went screaming off into the trees.'

'There was a dog, and a monkey,' said Sinclair wearily. 'It was a little circus act.'

'Probably copped it too,' said the sergeant, and pedalled on down the road, so slowly that it was a long time before Sinclair lost sight of him.

He walked on, but now he was only conscious of an infinite weariness and hurt, the reproachful ache in his mind that if they had not turned off the road for him they would still be alive, the old flute player and his mischievous little monkey, that rock-strong woman and her constant vivid shadow, the dog. Even the old horse who had rolled with such pleasure when released from the shafts, and the patient donkey – now all so needlessly, senselessly wiped out.

An hour later, as he turned from wary custom to look back along the road, he saw, less than a hundred yards behind, the furtive figure of a dog, slinking along on the verge. Sinclair stood stock still for a moment, his scalp prickling eerily. The dog stopped too, cowering. A tiny face with anxious eyes and wrinkled brows peered over the dog's head.

They were not ghosts conjured up by his uneasy mind; they were disconcertingly real. They looked very small and defenceless and tragic against this empty background. But their sudden return to life disturbed too deeply; they belonged

28

to the dead, and there was no place for them in his life, no time or thought to spare for them in their plight.

The dog crept forward, then hesitated, his ears laid back, his eyes showing recognition, the short tail quivering almost imperceptibly, but the soldier returned no recognition; turning abruptly, he continued on his way without a backward glance. He forced them out of his mind as determinedly as he forced his pace, for the mellow light of late afternoon lay over the land now.

The booming orchestration of the coastal guns ahead swelled and died away in longer and longer intervals. Somewhere a cow bellowed, and was answered by the lighter muffled call of a calf. A kestrel hovered over the far hedgerow, but swifts dipped and wheeled unheeding, low over the open field. A countryman all his life until he had shed his keeper's tweeds for a uniform in 1939, the soldier subconsciously noted these things, marked the distant returning rooks, flapping in a strange purposeful silence this day, the evening voices of all birds subdued. Stirred perhaps by the desire to see and hear such nostalgic commonplace in his own countryside again he quickened his pace, holding the webbing of the rifle away from the raw ache of his ribs. Behind him the dog stretched out too to maintain its imposed distance.

Nearer the town he saw a lone raider unload a stick of bombs across a field under the harassment of a diving Spitfire. He crossed the field afterwards in a short cut. The last bomb had straddled the hedge, scooping a crater deep into the soft sands of the rabbit warrens there. The blast must have blown the rabbits out of their burrows like shells from the muzzle of a gun. They lay in a sickle-shaped cluster about twenty feet from the crater's rim, outwardly whole and unharmed, as though dropped there by some retrieving dog. One doe, either at the moment of parturition, or as the result of blast propulsion, lay with a foetus between her hind legs, its sac already shrivelled by the sun, yet still intact, closely shrouding the miniature within.

29

Sinclair stopped, unable to tear his eyes away for a moment. On the far side of the crater the dog suddenly appeared, standing utterly still, his head up as though pulled back by the monkey's hands around his throat. Two pairs of eyes stared unwaveringly at him. It was as though they drew him down to their plight and size, so that he was in proportion to the animals dead and alive of this little ruined crater world. This raw wound in the earth which exposed the roots of a tree like entrails, this scattering of small limp bodies, the aborted doe – all was suddenly an unendurable desecration. The roots of one scrubby pine among a hundred pines, some twenty of the most prolific vermin dead – yet somehow a blasphemy so incomprehensibly terrible that he felt quite giddy and shaken.

In a sudden blind rage he shouted and swore at the dog, threatening with upraised arm, desperate to drive it away, to be rid of those remorselessly reminding eyes. *They must not follow him, hopelessly, uselessly, into the seaport. They must find some other human association – some farmhouse sanctuary perhaps.* 'Get out!' he yelled. 'Go back! Go away. . . . Shoo. . . . *Allez!*' He picked up a stone, feinted a throw to no effect. He threw it, deliberately short. The monkey buried its head, but the dog crouched steadfast, its eyes unwavering.

It was useless. He was wasting energy. Once more he turned his back resolutely, and set off at such a cathartic pace that he reached the outskirts of St Nazaire shortly before sunset. Only then did he look back. They were still there. But in the town centre he lost his followers at last. In the empty streets of blind-shuttered houses and shops, he took cover for a while against the falling flak. He saw the dog momentarily, obviously terrified by the barrage, cowering against a wall; then, as shrapnel rained down he bolted from cover, and the last Sinclair saw of him was the little grey form streaking away down the cobblestones, veering wildly, the dark shape of the rider crouched low to the outstretched neck. Sinclair pressed himself further into the stone arch of a garden wall, feeling at once both disquiet and relief to see them go. They had been incongruous enough before, but here their pathetic jockey-and-steed comicality was almost an outrage before the human tragedy of a war-torn town. Behind the shuttered windows of the house beyond, a crackling radio blared the Marseillaise.

The bombardment increased. It was dark before the first lull fell and he found his way to the military control post. The blacked-out town was still full of troops, patiently awaiting embarkation orders, dim silent forms hunched on the kerbs now, or propped against walls, identifiable only by the occasional firefly glow of a furtive cigarette. He had a mug of coffee at a canteen operating in the crypt of a roofless church, considered reporting his wound but decided against it when an ambulance drove up to a first aid post and he saw what one medical corps orderly had to contend with single-handed. He joined a file of silent men converging on the docks towards the black bulk of a destroyer lying alongside, but the bombardment started up again, the destroyer slipped away, and the file scattered for shelter.

For hours he crouched within the sandbagged emplacement of a wrecked gun with a dozen or so other men. Among them he recognised the young Lancashire Fusilier, last seen on a bicycle's crossbar, his feet now forced back into unlaced boots, the collie crouched by his side. When the boy's head fell forward and he slept momentarily, the dog stretched across his knees, whining, pawing at his chest until he wakened. Sinclair offered him a cigarette. The boy had reached the beaches of Dunkirk to find the last of the rescue craft pulled out. The collie had been one of a pack of abandoned dogs still roaming the water's edge. It had attached itself to him, following him back on the tortuous retreat across France, by truck at first, then on a train until it was derailed, and after that on foot. When he had crossed the Loire the dog had swum behind. The boy would not abandon him now. Somehow he would get this dog back to England.

His tale sparked off an exchange of experiences over the last hectic weeks among the group. One man, a despatch rider, told how he had skidded off a sharp bend and into the ditch minutes before a German column had rolled by. The machine was wrecked, but when he had crawled through the hedge he had found, miraculously awaiting him in the field, a horse, unaccountably saddled and bridled. There was no sign of an owner. Knowing little more than one end of a horse from the other he climbed gratefully aboard this providential transport, and set off to regain his signals unit on a cross-country course which lasted for nearly a week. Eventually he ended up at La Boule and there, with much regret, he was dismounted.

Sinclair told something of the caravan and its entourage, and a voice to his left spoke of seeing a proper circus, a whole convoy of bright modern wagons and trailer cages, including two elephants, heading out of Paris.

The talk fell away and the group dozed fitfully. Unable to ease his ribs into any comfortable position, Sinclair remained awake. Taking a packet of cigarettes out of his pocket he came across the medicine bottle. The swig, small though it was, exploded in his head, then spread its remembered warmth through his veins. He drank to the generosity of the old man, and then to that fierce-eyed brave woman, now so culpably dead – and at that moment, almost as though summoned, he felt rather than saw the wraithlike presence of the dog. A nose touched his hand, then quested within his open battle dress blouse, moving over the binding there. He drew deeply on the cigarette and in the red glow saw the familiar shape of the dog's head, and the dark limpet blur that was the monkey. They had found him, the one tenuous link with their destroyed past; their claim still strong in her scent on the strip of clothing around his ribs, and from her hands that had bound it there. The dog's eyes looked almost crazed with terror.

The man beside him flicked a shaded lighter. 'Cor,' he said, 'look what's here—' and a hand reached out to the monkey; but the dog whirled with bared teeth as the monkey gibbered fearfully and clung tighter. Another hand proffered a piece of chocolate, but the dog, trembling violently, pressed closer to Sinclair, thrusting his head into the shelter of his arm.

The monkey reached out to grab the edge of his blouse, then with a quick nervous decision thrust its head within. Sinclair knew nothing of monkeys, had never touched one before, and felt almost repelled by the dry warmth; but some instinct caused him to cup a hand over its haunches and the little thing burrowed in. He did up the buttons without a thought for the consequences of his action other than vaguely hoping that it would not sink its teeth in him later when he removed it. The black collie, ears pricked inquisitively, moved over to investigate, and the dog snarled. Lazily, Sinclair stretched out a proprietory leg and barred the collie with his boot, resting his hand reassuringly on the quivering dog – acknowledging the wrongness, the false premise of his responsibility even as he did so. He should have driven them off immediately.

When the order reached them to move he paused, his hand irresolute over the buttons. It was too small, too naked and human a burden to return to the shoulders of a small distraught dog. Even if he did so, it would not be easy to abandon or drive them away now that they had made contact; they had proved their tenacity. He buttoned up his blouse. The medicine bottle had made him quite lightheaded and carefree. Let them take their chance. Let someone else make the decision. Let some authority risk its fingers over the dislodgement of the monkey, the sharp attendant teeth of its guardian dog. He would not think further than the moment. He shared a last sip on French soil with the fusilier. 'Here's luck,' he said cheerfully, patting the almost imperceptible bulge on his chest.

The dog kept close to his heels. Ahead, groups of men were moving out of cover to the shaded pin prick of light that marked one gangway between the dock wall and the awaiting destroyer. As he drew nearer, he saw the collie running up and down the edge of the dock, gathering itself for a spring, hesitating, barking, running back to try again, and always failing before the ten-foot gap. As he awaited his turn to embark he saw that two MPs were stationed on either side of the gangway, and were turning back with well directed boots the frantic attempts of yet another dog to board.

He bent down and felt around the neck of the grey blur at his feet. The bell was firmly attached to some form of metallic thread but he silenced it by wrenching out the clapper. The next time he looked down his shadow was no longer there. He shuffled forward in his turn and produced his identifying paybook, feeling the small warm stillness under his pocket as he did so. A grey-faced naval officer, flanked by a keen-eyed Master of Arms, inspected his paybook briefly, glanced up at his face, then down to the front of his battle dress. Sinclair looked down too, resigned, expecting to find a tell-tale paw or tail sticking out, but 'Wounded?' asked the officer.

'Not seriously, sir,' said Sinclair.

'Report to the Medical Officer when you board the *Lancastria*,' said the officer, his eyes already on the man behind him.

As he boarded the gangway, Sinclair could just make out a small still form pressed against and merging into the canvas sides, only a few inches away from the gleaming boots of an MP. Between the boots and the canvas was a space of some eight inches, and he marvelled at the strategic positioning of this extraordinary little dog. Sure enough there was a momentary brushing, light as a feather, against the inside of one leg as he took the first step up the gangway, and at the end as he stepped down he felt it again.

It was impossible to move forward through the packed mass of humanity already on board the destroyer. His group was almost the last to be taken aboard before the gangway was removed. He remained jammed agonisingly against the rail as the destroyer slipped away from the dock and headed out to the great bulk of the liner that lay at anchor three miles out in the roadstead.

When they transferred to the *Lancastria*, it was impossible to distinguish anything at deck level among the milling boots in the darkness, but he had no doubt now that somewhere beyond the blue pin pricks of light in the dark cavern at the end of his second gangway crossing, his shadow would attach itself to him again.

Everything on board the liner was proceeding with calm efficiency. The *Lancastria's* crew remained as imperturbable as though the throngs of weary unwashed troops and ill-prepared civilians – women and children among them – and wounded were privileged passengers about to set off on a peacetime cruise. White-jacketed solicitous stewards were everywhere. He was directed where to report, where to collect a life-jacket, where to stow his kit; he was allocated a mattress in No. 2 hold, and even a time to appear in the dining saloon, and finally he was directed to the sick bay.

Up to this point, he had luxuriated only in being part of an unthinking process again. Now he had to force himself to make a personal decision, and his tired mind rebelled. A medical officer would obviously take a dim view of the monkey's unhygienic haven, and if he were once listed as wounded he would be caught up with medical officialdom the moment they landed in England. Was he really going to see this thing through? Was he really going to burden himself with the ultimate acceptance of transferred ownership? The smuggling ashore, the concealment? And then . . . ?

But the dark woman had not hesitated to accept responsibility for *him* . . .

Then scrub the sick bay, said Sinclair to himself, suddenly resolute. And scrub the mattress in No. 2 hold as well, he decided a minute later, feeling the strong revulsion of the countryman against the constraint of walls and packed humanity. The upper deck might be packed too with silent

35

huddled shapes, but above was the velvet night sky of June and fresh salt air. He made his way up and found a place beside a sleeping civilian at the end of a row of back-to-back seats; and even before he had wedged himself in, he was aware of a small shape slipping down the narrow tunnel formed at their base. After a while he put a hand down and smiled in satisfaction when he felt the touch of a nose. So far so good.

He had been handed two thick bully beef sandwiches soon after boarding. He ate one, then took the meat out of the other and passed it behind him, but it remained uneaten on the deck. He pushed a crust inside his blouse, but drew no response from the monkey. It seemed to be asleep. Sinclair closed his eyes and dozed uneasily.

When he woke they were anchored out in the searoads beyond St Nazaire. There was the promise of another still warm morning. The long low shape of Les Etoiles rose from the flat dawn sea to the west, and to the east lay the silent waiting coastline of France, plumes of black smoke rising lazily in the misty air. There was a suspenseful unreality about it, as of a backdrop to an empty stage vefore the play begins. On the *Lancastria*, reality lay in the spectators, in the grey unshaven faces of men huddled into ground sheets or gas capes against the dawn chill, and in the stirring unease that they were still there, a vulnerable audience for any show the enemy might care to put on.

Sinclair's immediate concern, however, was that the slight bulge at his chest was no longer there. He felt around in the folds of his blouse. The man beside him opened one eye. 'The monkey which is emerged from your vestments is now there—' he said in very French-accented English, and pointing vaguely behind him. 'It has sullied the floor,' he added severely. 'A sailor has expressed considerable chagrin.' He closed the eye.

Sinclair was relieved; at least it was not his vestments that had been sullied. The chagrined deckhand must have dealt with the offence for there was no sign. Nor was there any sign of the offender or the dog; they must be deep in the fastness of their tunnel. He decided to leave well alone and went off to queue up for a mug of tea and another sandwich.

On his way he saw the black collie of the night before, leaning possessively against a pack and rifle. A steward told him that he had seen at least a dozen other dogs on board, not to mention several cats, and a rabbit. And one of the army nursing sisters had even brought a tortoise along with her – he had managed to find some lettuce for that, he said proudly. He was obviously an animal lover, and his day was made when he heard about the monkey. He produced an apple and some raisins, and his final triumph was a packet of biscuits with raised bumps which he assured Sinclair were nuts. 'Come back here before we get to the other side,' he said. 'Once they're off the ship most of those animals will be collared by the officials – but there are ways . . .' He let the words fall significantly.

Fate seemed determined to steer his course, sending such a useful contact. Sinclair settled on a later rendezvous and made his way back. He had just emerged on to the upper deck when, almost simultaneously with the shipboard uproar of alarm bells and gongs and gunfire, there came the scream of aircraft engines. The liner shuddered convulsively to two nearby explosions, and men flattened on the deck like a pack of cards as the dark shapes passed over and veered off towards the coast before the barrage of gunfire. A choleric-faced Indian army major a few yards ahead of Sinclair lowered a hastily snatched rifle as he watched them go. 'I didn't lead them enough,' he said regretfully. 'Just wait till they come round again—' But the aircraft seemed to have been driven off for the moment; the ship's bells and a bugle rang the all clear soon afterwards. Men picked themselves up off the decks and resumed their grumbling, sunk back into lethargy, or went in search of a beer.

Too stiff and painful to bend down and peer along the seat

tunnel, Sinclair shoved the fruit and biscuits and a mug of water just inside. The animals must have been terrified by the explosions and gunfire, and he tried to entice them out with encouraging noises.

His seat mate gazed down with such raised eyebrows that he felt some explanation about how he had acquired his companions was due. The Frenchman was interested, and in his quaintly pedantic English was able to supply some background to those 'peoples of the roads' as he called them. They came from the Basque country to travel the sideroads and villages of France, as seasonal as the onion vendors, as shrouded in antiquity as the gypsies – possibly of Moorish blood, he thought. Sometimes singly, more often two or three wagons together, always with a small troop of performing dogs; and selling pegs and withy baskets as a side line. As a child in Brittany, he remembered seeing one with two dancing bears.

As the morning wore on and still the *Lancastria* lay at anchor the sense of unease deepened and spread from group to grumbling group. There was another raid at lunchtime, this time met with men's rifles and machine guns joining in with the ship's defences, and again driven off, but two miles away a black pall of smoke hung over their sister ship, the *Oronsay*. She had received a direct hit. It could have been them. Why didn't they push off now? At least, underway, they could take evasive action next time. What were they doing, tempting providence in this huge conspicuous liner out here in these shallow Loire waters? There were reportedly over six thousand troops and civilians aboard – true, every now and then another handful of weary men would be brought aboard from a fishing boat, but was that enough to justify the risk to six thousand lives? The silence from the coast became more and more oppressive, like the silence of a beast before it springs. Rumours spread: they were waiting for this, they were waiting for that; they would leave when the tide flooded, they were hemmed in by half the German navy; they were waiting for the rear guard to turn up, a naval escort, fighter aircraft escort; they were waiting to know where the hell *to* go, for England had been overrun as well . . .

As though sensing the unrest, the dog crept out of shelter at last and pressed shivering against Sinclair's knees; woebegone and bedraggled with terrified eyes and tucked-in tail, he was almost unrecognisable from the jaunty little leader of the caravan. Sinclair noticed that almost the entire left flank of the close curled coat had been singed. The monkey, on the other hand, seemed quite unscathed. It sat back on its haunches close to the dog, grimacing and rolling its lips back over its teeth between sips from the mug. It then emptied the remaining water over the dog's unflinching head and sidled swiftly up to a nearby soldier, newly woken, about to light a cigarette. Quick as a flash, the monkey grabbed his lighter, dropped it in the mug, then snatched the cigarette and stuffed it into its own mouth. Then, like a child showing off, the monkey rocked from one foot to the other and gibbered triumphantly as it waved the cup, wondrously preserving the lighter within and always tantalisingly out of reach of the owner.

He was a lighthearted diversion, and the men around cheered him on. After a while Sinclair clicked his fingers as he had seen the woman do and, to his surprise, the little creature came immediately, running crablike over the deck to reach up and offer the mug. He removed the lighter, restored it, and dropped in a franc instead. The monkey picked out the coin, bit it, and replaced it; then rattling the mug suggestively, importuned a row of men sitting on a Carley float. Good humouredly, they reached into their pockets and contributed.

Someone produced a mouth organ and began to play. The monkey jigged and hopped around and rattled the mug, deftly catching any pieces of chocolate or biscuit in the other paw – all of which he brought to Sinclair. The dog began to show a spark of interest; his eyes brightened, his ears crept up, and at last his tail unfurled as he watched. But the interlude was all too short; minutes later the music and voices were drowned

39

out by the Alert bells shrilling out again, while over the racket a voice came booming almost into their ears from a nearby Tannoy speaker: *'Action Stations! Action Stations! Take cover – take cover – take cover . . .'*

There was nowhere to take cover. Men flung themselves to the deck again, those who could crouched under the lifeboats or under the superstructure, others sheltered behind ventilating shafts, floats or seats, and monkey and dog fled back into their refuge tunnel. As the aircraft swept screaming towards them, the liner bucked to the blast of her own guns. Sinclair crouched at the end of the seats, saw the after Bofors gun swivelling and braced himself for another earsplitting round. Only a few feet away, two gunners had set up their machine gun and were already blazing away in company with scattered volleys of rifle fire. Above it all he heard the spaced whistle of an approaching stick of bombs, felt the ship shudder violently to each closer underwater explosion, and hunched himself tightly before the last wailing downward scream that filled his head to bursting point. As though scoring some Olympian goal the bomb dropped down the single funnel, exploding below the water line with such force that the *Lancastria* leaped like a mortally wounded animal, the jolting waves of her pain passing through every rivet of her length.

A still second of shocked acknowledgement followed, then the guns roared out again over the clang and rattle of falling flak and twisted red hot metal. The liner had listed sharply, then, as the sea surged in far below the water line she righted herself, wallowing in a sluggish roll that became increasingly ill-balanced. Under such a momentum, it could not be long before the more heavily listing side would lose, and then she would turn turtle. Sinclair reached for his lifejacket.

Clear above the bedlam of noise, a steady voice through a loud hailer directed men to remove their boots and clothes and jump now, for with the deck already beginning to tilt ominously, only the starboard lifeboats could be released. Within minutes the angle had become so steep that men, equipment, floats and seats avalanched together towards the rail.

Clinging on to the fixed seat as they kicked off their boots, Sinclair and the Frenchman waited until the area directly below was cleared; as they slithered down together the monkey leaped for his shoulder and clung tightly around his neck. The dog shot past, paws scrabbling without traction until halted by the raised combing beyond the rail.

'One, two, three, and over we go,' said Sinclair, as the other man hesitated by the rail.

'As yet I am unable to swim,' said the Frenchman in thin, precise tones, looking down with extreme distaste.

'You won't learn standing here,' said Sinclair. 'Here, put this on—' and he pulled at the tapes of his jacket, trying to wrench it off: but the limpet monkey had hold of his hair and clung on grimly.

The rail was within twenty feet of the water now. As he struggled to dislodge the monkey a lifeboat swung out on its davits a miraculous few yards away. There was a rush to fill it, but he steadied the Frenchman as the other climbed on to the rail and reached for the bows. He heaved, and the man was up and over and safely into the lifeboat.

From below in the water a face looked up, and a voice yelled: 'For God's sake, hold your jacket down when you go – I nearly dislocated my bloody neck—'

He was over the rail when he saw the dog, desperately balancing on the almost vertical edge. He scooped him up as he jumped. He knew that he must get as far away as possible from the sucking vortex that would follow when the ship went down. He was mad to hinder himself with the dog. He released his grip and started swimming, encumbered by the lifejacket and breathless with pain. The dog paddled along easily beside him.

Behind him a demented medley of noise escalated almost unendurably above the hiss of escaping steam and bells still jangling madly, whistles and shouts, and somewhere, muffled, an inhuman screaming, while overall the calm strong voice directed steadily from the loud hailer. Incredibly a machine gun was still firing. He heard the slapping crash as the lifeboat dropped free from the falls, and turning his head was suddenly aware that the monkey's arms were once more wrapped around his neck; it must have wedged itself in somehow between his back and the hump of the old-fashioned cork life-jacket when he jumped.

A spar of wood to which was still attached part of a cane seat suddenly bobbed up in front of him; he grabbed it and rested for a moment. The dog's paws churned as he tried to get some purchase on the wood and raise himself out of the water, and had almost succeeded when the spar rolled over. Choking on the salt water, he bobbed up again, his eyes wildly imploring, his paws beating ineffectually. Sinclair raised him by the scruff of his neck and rested the forepaws over his own forearm. If the dog had resisted him, used up too much of his small reserve of energy, he would have held its head underwater then and there and put an end to it; but almost as though recognising the possibility, the dog hung on without struggling.

Sinclair turned to watch the last mortal moments of the *Lancastria*. Her bows already under, men still retreating flylike up the stern, the great liner reared almost three-quarters of her length clear of the water, then slid with slow inexorable majesty to the depths, her siren still blaring, silenced only with a last hissing sigh of steam. The waters closed over her in a great swirling emptiness. Then heads bobbed up like corks, and debris erupted and boiled over the surface.

In the silence that followed, the shouts of one to another travelled clearly across the water. Over the flat horizon that was now his, Sinclair saw an assorted local fleet of fishing boats and launches converge on the area; beyond them, two small cargo ships had altered course, while further away to the south he could make out the bow wave of a destroyer heading towards them.

The water was cold, but he felt confident that he would be picked up soon – provided that enemy aircraft had the decency not to return and shoot up the survivors. And provided that he had the strength to swim out of reach of the oil, he thought more urgently as he saw the first viscid blackness float up and begin to spread, edged widely in places by the shining silver of shoals of dead fish.

The grasp of the wood was comforting; he turned away from the oil slick and paddled towards the distant destroyer against the light wind. Presumably crouched on the life-jacket at the back of his neck, the monkey was burdenless and un-demanding, almost non-existent. As long as it stayed that way it could remain there. He shifted the dog's paws to a better purchase on the cane seat and pushed on.

Other men had had the same idea of turning into the wind in the hope of outmanoeuvring the oil, and now there was a steady, slow, almost organised movement; the helpless and helpers were sorting themselves out. Sometimes one of the strong single swimmers catching up from behind shared his spar for a brief rest. An empty lifeboat floated by, men clinging to the looped ropes on her sides.

A small crate, empty and very buoyant, both ends stove in, followed. He caught it, shoving the spar through until the seat jammed against the sides so that the spar now rode fairly steadily. He gave the dog a slight heave, so that it gained the half-submerged seat and it crouched there shiver-ing. At this, the monkey leaped on to the crate top, clear of the water.

Among the bobbing heads before him, he could make out those of two other dogs. One paddled in aimless splashing circles. The other, obviously a large and powerful animal, was rapidly closing the gap to its target, a man without a life-jacket holding on to some partially submerged piece of flot-sam. Powerless to intervene at this distance, Sinclair watched as the dog caught up and made frantic clawing attempts to climb on to the man's back. Despite his struggles, the weight on his shoulders forced the man's head below water time and time again. He was probably a non-swimmer, for it was all over in a few minutes, and the head went down for the last time. The dog swam on, searching for another foothold, and as it turned in his direction Sinclair reached in his pocket for a knife, but the first few feet of a wide ribbon of oil intervened. The dog tried to board this apparently solid surface, gulped oil in its panic, and shortly after its head disappeared too.

The oil when it reached him spread over in a vile viscid embrace, coating the spar so that his hands slipped off, and for a moment it drifted smoothly ahead, its occupants staring back in bleak anguish until he caught up with them. The dog tried to scramble up beside the monkey on the crate top, still clear of oil. The crate rocked wildly; somehow the monkey hung on, but the dog's paws slipped and he fell back. For a moment it all seemed too hopeless to try and sort out again; it was as much as he could do to hang on to the spar himself and keep his mouth clear of oil. Then, despite himself, he bent his elbow under the haunches, and with this purchase to the hind legs the dog scrambled back on to the cane seat, the gleaming blue-black oil plastering his coat all except the head. After many attempts, and hardly knowing why he did so, Sinclair undid one of the tapes of his life-jacket and passed it under the spar and back, where he knotted it again securely.

Another lifeboat went by, dangerously low in the water, packed with men, the ropes festooned with others. 'What happened to your hurdy-gurdy, mate?' someone called. Then, 'Hang on, lad,' called another, 'plenty of boats picking up now.'

He could see them, the launches and lifeboats and whalers of the destroyer and other ships, zigzagging to and fro as they picked up survivors. But none came his way, although he waved and shouted. Later he was thankful for his apparent invisibility, for the enemy aircraft returned, machine-gunning where the survivors and boats were thickest, and dropping incendiaries in an attempt to ignite the oil. Mercifully the flames only flickered briefly into life.

The remaining heads were widely scattered now, none within earshot; he missed being within range of the shouts of encouragement one to another, and the silence was beginning to be so oppressive that he spoke words of reassurance to the animals from time to time if only to hear his own voice. He found himself envying their animal ability to take whatever came without protest, to go with it somehow, and turn themselves off into an almost trance-like state with half-closed withdrawn eyes. Yet every time he spoke, the dog turned his head and gave him his full regard, with eyes as suddenly alert as though blinds had sprung back.

Sinclair seemed to have drifted further and further away from the rescue ships on the horizon, and as the lonely hours wore on he became increasingly weak and at times light-headed. His legs were numb with cold, and he knew that he must keep moving them, but all effort to propel his spar towards that distant goal of the destroyer had become excruciating.

The monkey seemed to be shrinking, grey and cold; he wondered vaguely, but without real concern, how long it could survive. It looked impossibly fragile, eyes closed, and huddled into its own enwrapping arms. But as he rested for a moment, it suddenly reached down and touched his eyebrow, withdrawing its fingers to examine the oil on them closely, sniffed them, plainly did not like the smell, and wiped them delicately on its as yet unplastered chest.

The dog crouched only inches before him, the oil-slicked coat sculpturing bone and muscle to shining blue-black relief, the eyes no longer half-closed, but wide and alive, always riveted on his now, so close as to reflect him within the pupils like twin convex mirrors. There were times when he felt the effort needed to hold on was too much, that it would be so much simpler just to let go and drift off into peaceful oblivion. Then always, just as his will was slipping away, he would be jerked back to open his eyes and see himself again in those other intent summoning ones.

Then came a moment of sharp lucidity, returning from a pleasant drifting dream, and he suddenly knew at last that the tiny black face with the red-rimmed eyes was real, it was *himself;* and the moment he no longer saw himself there, he would no longer see any of the things he held most dear in the world either. He must stay wakeful and cling on to the spar, to life – even as these animals clung to their precarious raft; they might *appear* to have withdrawn from the situation behind shuttered eyes, but he saw now that their bodies were always controlled, and tensed to balance, to survival. Once again, his world was circumscribed to their small one.

'All right,' he said aloud, and taking the monkey's nearest paw he wiped his eyes clear with it. 'All right, lads,' he repeated with louder determination as both heads turned towards him. 'Here we go – hold on, everyone, we're *off.*' He kicked his legs until some circulation returned, took a firmer grasp on the slimy spar and swam on.

He was almost unconscious but his legs still fractionally moving, robot-like, his eyes fixed wide open, when the dog began to bark. It was a high, piercing bark, but even that did not penetrate his mind; nor did a voice when it called out, very close above his head; his legs continued to move. Only when another voice said, 'Cut that jacket free—' did he rouse into sudden wideawake panic, seeing the descending knife, the severance from his known world. He fought desperately for sensibility, but all that his voice would utter above the barking was 'No, no, no . . .'

At last he forced a complete sentence out. 'Grab the dog,' he said and tried to take the scruff of the slimy black neck himself, but his fingers slipped. A pair of arms reached out and hauled him so that he lay half over the combing of the boat, resting in agony on crunching ribs before he finally slithered over, the pain forcing his breath out in shallow gasps. Someone wiped his mouth and eyes clear of oil, and eased off the cumbersome jacket. The whaler was filled with other slumped figures, black shining faces, red lips, red eyes, and from all around came the harsh racking sounds of retching and coughing from oil-filled stomachs and lungs. From these blacknesses, a small blackness detached itself and crawled to his side. He clung on to it in sudden fierce protectiveness and, still clinging, dropped off into unconsciousness at last.

Part Two

4

Sick Berth Attendant Neil MacLean, of H.M. destroyer *Tertian*, was tending a group of walking wounded on deck when word reached him that the ship's whaler had been swung aboard and that there was a man haemorrhaging in it. He called for a stretcher, and made his way forward, pressing urgently through the jammed mass of soldiers. Only two men were left in the whaler. The one who lay stretched in the stern sheets, one leg at a grotesque angle with a blood-soaked jacket under it, was obviously the haemorrhage for someone had twisted a belt around his thigh as a tourniquet. MacLean sent him as an emergency to the wardroom where the ship's doctor was working with the help of an RAMC Captain.

He turned his attention to the other man, the front of his battle dress stained bright recent red, a matching trickle running from his mouth. He bent down to take the man's pulse and his fingers suddenly came in contact with a warm slimy black mass below the hand, so horrible in its unexpectedness that instinctively he withdrew his fingers. Part of the black mass split open to red and gleaming white, and a low warning snarl preceded the snapping together of the white gleam.

'*A'thiaghrna!*' said MacLean, reverting aloud in the reflex of relief and surprise to his native Gaelic. The man's eyes opened in the blackness of his face and he answered in the same tongue: 'Leave the dog be,' he whispered. 'I'll leave him all right,' said MacLean with a sour look at the sharp

51

teeth so close to his hands as he investigated the wound below the blouse. 'I need my hands the day.'

The man struggled to sit up, but the effort brought an ooze of scarlet froth to his lips.

'Stay where you are,' said MacLean sharply, and called back for another stretcher. But the soldier suddenly strained up in such wild incoherence that MacLean had to hold him down. Now the man's words came in such panting distress that MacLean felt certain one lung must have been pierced by a rib fragment. 'The animals – where were they?"

'Resting – lying back *resting*,' said MacLean smoothly, thinking that this one would be resting eternally himself very soon if he didn't lie still and stop torturing the remaining lung. He felt in his satchel for an ampule.

'The horse—' panted the soldier, barely audible. 'The rabbits – *all* those rabbits, they were innocent – I tell you, they were *innocent* . . . even the bear.'

'All having a nice wee rest the now,' crooned MacLean hypnotically as he slid in the needle.

The man's eyes closed but they shot open again wildly when they came to move him to a stretcher. His hand groped to his side and across his chest, searching.

'All right, all right,' said MacLean. 'Lie still, for Christ's sake, the dog's there – no one's going to take it away.'

He stood up; there were others awaiting him. He looked at the throng of naked exhausted bodies and, as though summoned, a man, fully clothed, clean and dry, eased through them and squatted down beside the stretcher.

'It is I,' he announced formally, and the soldier's eyes opened and crinkled in recognition.

'You know him?' said MacLean, and the man nodded.

'Keep him from moving, then, until the drug takes effect. Rub his legs, and try and keep him warm – and watch out, there's a dog underneath the blanket—'

'Yes,' said the helper, already busy. '*And* that one – *le singe*,' he added, cocking an eye at a point above. MacLean looked too; on the superstructure, twenty feet above, was the tiny huddled figure of a monkey, one hand doubled loosely on its knee, the other stuffed in its mouth, its eyes fixed on the head of the dog below. At least there was no sign of the soldier's other innocents, the decks so far clear of horse or rabbits. MacLean departed.

An hour later he returned. The drug had done its work and the soldier drowsed. The Frenchman had managed to ease off his oil-soaked battle dress, and had cleaned him up. The dog lay close by on the battle dress blouse. Up to this point, the man on the stretcher had been just another glistening black mask with white and red cut-outs for mouth and eyes. Now MacLean looked down on a face that shock and bloodlessness had etched to its finest point, the fine, pale clear-skinned face, black hair and dark blue eyes of the west Highlander. The soldier tried to speak, but went into an agonising spell of coughing.

MacLean kneeled down and held him until it was over. He spoke softly, persuasively, in Gaelic. 'Wheesht, man, wheesht,' he said, 'and give your lungs a chance. Save your breath for breathing.' He laid him down at the end of the paroxysm and, kneeling there, smiled reassuringly; a smile that transformed his tired, lined face with its grim, set mouth.

The soldier's lips moved again. As he whispered, the dog crept on its belly to the head of the stretcher, there to lay its muzzle on the edge.

'I will do his talking,' said the dry precise voice of the Frenchman as MacLean worked swiftly to change the dressing. 'He wishes to tell you that he is not wounded, that he must walk off this ship, for he has these two companions who have come a long way with him. They have no one else apparently. He is obsessed. They are a trust. He must walk off, for if he goes to hospital he will be separated from them, and this is insupportable.'

The dog lifted its head, and its inflamed eyes under the matted hair looked directly into MacLean's, only a few inches away, almost as though waiting to hear his comment. Mac-Lean shifted his gaze, and found that the soldier's eyes now held his, no longer unfocussed but holding an agony of waiting comprehension. He had seen this look too often that day; sometimes it was heralded with a thin, barely perceptible then leaping pulse – then all too often the pulse stopped for ever. 'Ach, don't fash yourself so, man,' said MacLean. He continued with cheerful professional mendacity. 'No need to worry – you just leave it all to us.'

'I have your hand on it?' the soldier managed to whisper. His hand moved on the blanket, and the dog stretched forward to touch it with his muzzle. '*Am bheil do làmh agam airansin?*'

But there was a difference between the professional assurance, and the binding promise of his word; for a moment MacLean hesitated. The dog's intense, uncomfortably human eyes watched him. A voice shouted urgently for him, and he rose. The dog rose too, still watching. The words were forced out of him it seemed. 'Aye,' he said, 'I'll see to him, never you fear. *Mo làmh air an sin.* You have my hand on it. Now rest, will you—'

He passed by several times that night, each time half-expecting to find the blanket pulled over the man's face, but he seemed to be sleeping, and his pulse was stronger. The Frenchman was nodding beside him, only the dog watchful and suspicious as he bent over the stretcher.

At one point, as he turned back the blanket, he found the monkey curled into an incredibly small tight ball between the soldier's arm and chest, its head buried deeply. MacLean's lips pursed with displeasure, but the dog growled fiercely when he tried to move it. He left well alone – let it go ashore on the stretcher undetected; he wished the medical orderlies joy in its discovery. His promise had been for the dog alone. With that in mind late in the afternoon, his hand descended with practised skill upon its muzzle; he deftly inserted two or three pills down an instantly submissive throat, and dropped a jacket over it. The rails were lined with silent watching

54

men as the shores of England loomed out of the mist. It would not be long before they disembarked. He would return for his bundle in good time. He made a careful note of the details in the soldier's paybook.

Two weeks before, the British Expeditionary Force had been taken off the Dunkirk beaches in the most glorious makeshift fleet ever assembled off the coast of England, a fleet that steamed, sailed, waddled and chugged its way across the Channel, and once home, barely waited to disembark its troops before returning for more. Reception in England was of necessity often as makeshift, and in the confusion and urgency quite a few Fifth Columnists and other undesirables had infiltrated with the returning troops.

But by the time *Tertian* docked at Falmouth with the *Lancastria*'s survivors, certain aspects of security had been tightened up. Outwardly it was the same: the fleet of ambulances drawn up on the quayside, the Salvation Army doughnuts and tea, the lines of tired men shuffling off the gangways past the Military Police and the lynx-eyed security officers of the different services, then forming into groups to be detailed off to billets or transport. But this time, having learned the lesson that its four-footed camp followers will trail the British Army, even in retreat, the Port Health and Quarantine officials were ready for them. A man with a large net on the end of a pole was stationed beside the police; an RSPCA van stood waiting, and any suspiciously-shaped packs were being examined.

The last of the wounded ashore, the wardroom already cleared of dressings and surgical instruments, Neil MacLean leaned for a few minutes' respite over *Tertian*'s rail and watched the scene below. He saw an angry cat removed from a gas mask haversack, while several dogs that he had not even seen aboard were lead off to the van; a mynah bird, perched on an Air Force officer's finger, laughing in some falsetto imitation, passed the inspection triumphantly; so did a mandarin drake, its head sticking out inquisitively from a pillowcase under the arm of one of the women civilian survivors, now wearing a pair of seaman's trousers and a violently striped sweater that MacLean recognised as belonging to the doctor. But something that looked like a ferret or a white rat, which gave itself away by peering out of the blanket folds around the neck of one of the walking wounded was plucked out gingerly, despite its owner's protestations that it was British born and was only coming home like him.

There had been no inspection of the stretcher cases, however: as long as that monkey remained curled in the recumbent ball he had last seen, it would have made it safely ashore. He watched the loaded ambulances speeding off with some satisfaction; the soldier had been in one of the first to go, MacLean having seen to that early in the morning by marking a priority on his medical tag. The man had been unconscious then, his breathing so rasping and laboured that it hurt even to listen to it.

Only minutes before, the helpful Frenchman had waved back as he went down the gangway. Drawn aside from the lines, he was still being interrogated by two men in plain clothes. Presently, they escorted him to a shed that was closely guarded, MacLean noticed, regretting that he would never know what merited this attention – VIP or aspiring German agent?

He heard the wailing message of the bo'sun's pipe summoning all hands to clean ship. The decks were a slippery shambles of oil-covered clothes, blankets and rags and life-jackets, the paintwork covered with a ghostly frieze of naked black silhouettes and handprints. He turned to go, yawning, longing to get his head down and his eyes closed if only for a few minutes before he started in on his own section below. A small smacking noise attracted his attention; ten feet above his head, huddled dismally on the inner ring of a life-buoy hanging over the bridge rail, was the monkey. It smacked its lips again softly and looked for a moment as though it were about to jump down on to his shoulder.

MacLean scowled up at it, furious that it had outwitted him.

The monkey moved listlessly along the rail, squeaking softly, was lost to view, then a second later appeared at the bottom of the companionway and timidly inched towards him, so close now that he could see the rings of oil around the inflamed eyes. Almost within his reach, it stretched out a paw as trustingly as a child – and at that moment the quayside siren, almost directly alongside, started on its first wailing crescendo and was matched by *Tertian*'s action stations alarm. The monkey fled, swarming up a stay, fouling the deck as it went. MacLean gazed gloomily after. He turned through the steel doorway and clattered down to the sick bay.

The doctor had gone ashore with some of the wounded. The cabin reeked, and looked as though a hurricane had hit it. He opened the scuttle wide, took off his jacket and rolled up his shirt sleeves. It was very quiet now that the hurrying feet throughout the ship had settled down into the waiting silence of action stations, the flat outside the door and the cabins leading off were deserted. He was safe from interruption at least until the All Clear sounded again; nevertheless he drew the door curtain across.

From the cupboard under the bunk, he drew out a cardboard box marked Boracic Lint and turned back the brown paper lying on top. Inside, on an evil-smelling oily blanket, eyes closed, but with its flanks moving steadily up and down, was the dog. The heavy sedative that he had given it would ensure that it remained this way for several more hours – by which time he hoped that he might have some more inspiration as to its future.

He threw the blanket on a pile in the corner, lifted out the limp bundle and laid it on a rubber sheet on the bunk. Then with swift thoroughness he went to work with swabs, surgical spirit and detergent. Towelling the result dry, he looked down on the small body presently with professional satisfaction. The coat was revealed as a closely curled blue-grey, the hair singed off in a large area on one flank, and down to the flesh on a raw burn at the root of the short tail. This was dressed with the same meticulous care as the eyes had been bathed and the ears swabbed out. He looked with a critical eye at the lines of the dog.

It had all the proportion and apparent fragility of bone that suggested some poodle blood at first sight; but the hind-quarters were exceptionally powerful and there was an unusual depth of chest; there was the high-domed forehead that he usually associated with present-day overbreeding – and stupidity to go with it, but this enigmatic dog had an unexpected width between the eyes. The muzzle was short, clean cut and pointed. He pulled back the black lips and examined the teeth: shining white, but very slightly worn, and he decided that the dog must be around seven years old. A slight parting in the damp mat of hair around the neck caught his attention: close against the skin below was a strand of ribbon through which ran a single metallic thread, dull now under the oil. He cut it off, finding that it ran through the ring of a tiny silver bell with the clapper missing. He dropped the ribbon into a basin of solvent, wiped it off, and put it in his pocket.

The All Clear went, and he was galvanised into swift action. Scooping up the dog, he wrapped it in a dry towel, then laid it in the middle of the soiled pile, covering it loosely. Activity returned to the ship; descending boots clattered, voices rang out. He drew back the curtain and was hard at work when the first figures passed by the open door.

Now that he was irrevocably embarked on his course, he no longer felt tired, but almost exhilarated. The outline of his immediate strategy was already formulated; his promise would be fulfilled. In due course, he would ship the dog back to the soldier – but that lay in the future, and there was no point in wasting present thought on the unpredictable. Equally his mind shied off superstitiously from the thought that he might have the animal on his hands for good if its owner died.

His present plan was based on his guess that they would return to sea the moment the ship was re-fuelled. Falmouth was too vulnerable for one thing, and for another every ship would be needed against the possibility of invasion. As long as *Tertian* left within the next few hours, everything would be all right; once they were at sea he could count on the sentiment that would arise over such a defenceless stowaway. And fortunately the precedent of animals aboard had already been set in *Tertian*: from the supreme level of the captain's bull terrier, who had been with the ship from the day she was commissioned, down to Hyacinthe, the ship's cat, a matriarchal tortoiseshell with six toes to her front paws, who reigned over the lower decks. And the same maudlin sentiment would go for that damned monkey too, he thought; let the crew once make contact with that – if it had enough sense to stay out of reach until they sailed – and it would be home free too. Just so long as he, Neil MacLean, SBA, took care – a proceeding which came easily to him – to see that nothing could be pinned on him in connection with their appearance, he was home free too . . .

By the time the MO had returned, he had everything gleaming and shipshape, and was seated at the desk filling in forms. Apart from the stained pile by the door, the sick bay wore its usual look of impersonal shining efficiency. The doctor congratulated him, and told him to turn in for a couple of hours while he could – as the buzz was that they would cast off as soon as they had been at least partially revictualled, the *Lancastria*'s survivors having cleaned them out.

MacLean asked him a few questions about the shore evacuation of the wounded – the RASC corporal, Sinclair, with the lacerated lung who had been on the first ambulance? He was pretty far gone, the doctor remembered; in fact, they had rushed him off to a local hospital instead of the hospital train.

'Was he anyone you knew?' he asked MacLean absently, scrawling his signature on papers.

'No, sir,' said MacLean, 'Never seen him in my life before.

Came aboard with a little dog and a monkey they tell me, after hours in the drink too.'

'Good grief,' said the doctor, yawning hugely. 'What happened to them?'

'Probably got ashore with the troops,' said MacLean, 'and then picked up by Quarantine – they tell me that there were quite a few animals on board this trip. If you would just be signing these as well, sir, and then if you will not be wishing anything further, I will be taking this lot ashore.'

He tied the four ends of a sheet around the bundle by the door, put on his cap, picked up the bundle, fastidiously wiped off a speck of oil on the gleaming bulkhead and prepared to depart. His face was white with exhaustion and he suddenly looked very old to the young doctor.

'Go and get your head down, man, and to hell with that lot,' he said. 'And that's an order – just lose it in the sullage barge, or overboard, we'll indent for more.'

'We already have, sir,' said MacLean primly, and departed.

He took the bundle down to the mess which he shared with the acting petty officers and some of the victualling staff, slinging a hammock there when the destroyer was in port. At sea, he slept in the sick bay, and wished he were there now, with a comfortable cot, and that handy concealing cupboard underneath it.

The mess was deserted except for APO Reid who was trying to clear the decks of acrid treacly litter. MacLean did not trouble to conceal anything from this one man; Reid was a close-mouthed individual. He slid the towel-wrapped bundle of dog out on the deck, turned back an edge to reassure himself, then lifted it into the bottom of his locker. After checking that the ventilation slits at the bottom were not blocked, he locked the door.

'What you got there – Moses?' asked Reid.

'A dog,' said MacLean.

'Looks dead,' observed Reid, fishing a pair of braces and three socks out from under the table.

'Doped,' said MacLean sitting down, and distastefully stubbing out a smouldering cigarette stub.

Reid threw an army boot on to his stack and looked sceptical.

'See here,' said MacLean, rare persuasion in his voice, 'you never saw it – neither did I. When we're at sea, it appears and that's that – something else left behind by the pongos. No one's going to heave a poor wee dog like that overboard, is he?'

'Wouldn't put it past the Buffer,' said Reid, referring to the Master at Arms who was reputed to have a copy of King's Regulations instead of a heart, 'nor yet the First Lieutenant,' he went on. 'He carried on something awful when Hyacinthe had that litter in his bunk.'

'It was very careless he was,' said MacLean severely. 'He should have kept his door shut.'

'You might get it as far as Devonport,' admitted Reid, 'but then what? You'll be up on a charge if you're caught smuggling it ashore. What do you want a dog for anyway?'

'*I* don't want a dog,' said MacLean sourly. 'That would be the last thing I would be wanting.'

'You must be barmy,' said Reid. 'Who's so important anyway that you'd take the risk?'

Useless to explain his quixotic promise to this hard-headed Yorkshireman what he could not put into words himself even – that he and that wounded soldier shared a common tongue and heritage, that their birthright alone imposed an obligation. 'I'm doing it for a kinsman,' he said simply, 'and Devonport's a fair way off yet. I might need a hand – there would be a pint or two in it,' he added cautiously.

Reid stirred his heap with the toe of his boot. 'I'll not risk a stripe,' he said at last, 'and I haven't seen anything, but within limits – would there be a meal thrown in with the pints perhaps?'

'Aye, there would be that,' agreed MacLean. 'I can count on you, then?'

'Aye, you can that,' said Reid, imitating the soft inflection, so that MacLean flushed angrily, was about to say something, thought better of it and went off to try and scrounge a mug of tea out of the galley before cleaning up the wardroom.

'Didn't you do some kind of work with animals in civvy street?' asked the assistant cook, who was one of his messmates. 'Do you know anything about monkeys?'

'A bit,' said MacLean cautiously.

'Then you'd better get up to the foredeck,' said the cook. 'There's one there and they can't get it down. The Chief's in a proper tear about it—'

Armed with some nuts, MacLean made his way up to the foredeck. The monkey was clinging to a stay. The Chief Petty Officer was directing two ratings to its capture, and there was a lot of encouraging banter from the rest of the work party. It looked infinitely small and pitiful, the skin loosely shrivelled, the oil streaked face so pinched and furrowed that it had almost retreated into the frame of fur. MacLean had intended to do nothing about it, to leave it to the crew to find; now he realised that the vital spark that had kept this delicate creature going so miraculously long in nightmare conditions would be extinguished if something were not done soon. This could not be allowed.

As he joined the ring of men, the monkey's head turned towards him. 'Tch, tch, tch,' he said and recognition came into the eyes, the black upper lip drew back from its teeth and he heard the soft smacking sounds of greeting. It reached out an arm towards him.

'All right, you have a go, MacLean' said the Chief disgustedly. 'You try and get the little perisher down.'

MacLean held out his hand, palm upwards, with the nuts. The monkey dropped down at once and scuttled to his feet where it grasped a trouser leg and gazed earnestly up at his face. It put out a hesitant paw, then took a few nuts, stuffing them listlessly into its mouth with forefinger and thumb. The watching group to a man admired this prodigious feat with sentimental smiles, and even the Chief's face relaxed for a moment before he recollected himself and told one of the ratings to grab it. But the monkey huddled against MacLean's leg, clinging on, and threatened with lips pulled back over its teeth when the hand approached. The hand retreated smartly.

'Come along now, Wainwright,' said the Chief. 'Smartly now, before the First Lieutenant comes along and says what the fricking hell's going on on my foredeck.'

The sailor straightened up and looked at him. He was a giant of a man who looked not unlike a gorilla. 'I'm afraid, Chief,' he said gravely, and there was a snigger from the men.

'You have a go, Chiefie,' they said encouragingly, and the Chief bent down – then retreated sharply before the teeth.

Suddenly the monkey took things into his own paws; reaching up for MacLean's hand, it swung itself up into the crook of his arm and clung around his neck. It was shivering, yet there was a dry heat to its body that MacLean's mind associated immediately with other ailing monkeys in other days.

'Right,' said the Chief Petty Officer briskly. 'Now, MacLean, if you'll just double off to the Harbour Police with it, and you, Wainwright, swab that mucky deck down, we'll get on with the job of running this ship—' but the last of his words were drowned by the wail of sirens and, as the ship's alarm bells followed, the group scattered to their stations. The monkey burrowed its head deeply into MacLean's jacket, trying to shut out the din.

'Hang on to it, MacLean,' bellowed the Chief against the uproar. 'Get it below and . . .'

As MacLean ducked in through the steel doorway, he saw the anti-aircraft gun mounted on the superstructure above already swivelling around. He covered the monkey's head with his hand, pressing it against his shoulder before the ensuing noise. It rewarded him by vomiting down his jacket.

The doctor was still sitting in the sick bay, his feet on the desk, his eyes closed. MacLean coughed gently. 'The Chief sent me down with one of the *Lancastria*'s lot that got left behind, sir,' he said.

The doctor opened his eyes and took in the monkey without any change of expression. 'The army's really scraping the bottom of the barrel, isn't it?' he observed at last. 'What is it, and what's it complaining of?'

'A capuchin monkey, sir, suffering from exposure and possible pneumonia,' said MacLean with equal gravity.

The doctor sighed, removed his feet from the desk, and took a stethoscope out of the drawer. 'Take a deep breath, capuchin,' he said. Then as the monkey bared its teeth, '*Your* patient, I think, MacLean,' he added generously, and watched with sleepy interest as the patient submitted apathetically to having its eyes swabbed out, drops administered and M & B tablets crushed up in water and poured down its throat without a drop being spilled. Finally it was briskly and neatly cocooned in cotton wool and a towel. 'Very professional,' he said approvingly, 'and now what?'

'No. 1 boiler room,' said MacLean as he departed, with a look of such profound distaste at the bundle in his arms that he might have been bent on incineration rather than its eventual installation in a cardboard box with some holes punched out in the lid.

Three hours later, *Tertian* cast off from the tanker and slipped away from Falmouth, heading for the open Atlantic, her complement irrevocably increased by two small and very miserable refugees.

5

In the circumstances they could not have been more fortunate. *Tertian* was what was known in the Navy as a 'happy ship': from the day that she had been commissioned, her officers and men had shaken down and integrated to form the mysterious chance medley that makes such a ship, and into which two more animals were easily assimilated. Besides, she was only fulfilling the role of her familiar alias 'Noah's Ark' – a nickname that had followed inevitably when Lieutenant Commander Andrew Knorr, RN had been appointed to her command – as the shipboard sages pointed out.

As well as being the 'Owner' of his Ark and a flaming red beard, Knorr was also the owner of the legendary Barkis, some seventy amiable pounds of solid white bull terrier who had conformed to life in a destroyer almost as though he had evolved there. Even his descent of a vertical ladder or companionway was a fine bold adaptation: with forelegs in diving position and hind legs extended, his mighty body steeled, he would hurl himself down the length as though on a chute, gaining such impetus on the way that he usually slithered several feet along the deck, taking the legs away from anyone unfortunate enough to be in his path as he went. While the ship's company admired and respected their skipper for qualities such as unruffled seamanship or his unique – and contagious – general enthusiasm, it was quite obvious that Barkis regarded him merely as a willing, easily taken-in slave.

When Knorr eventually issued an official warning, therefore, that any subsequent infringement of ship's discipline that could be traced to the presence of the new arrivals on board would result in their being dumped overboard forthwith (an operation that he, personally, would supervise), no one was unduly alarmed.

The dog had been discovered in a store room, most fortuitously by none other than APO Reid, who duly reported its presence to the Buffer, receiving the sole comment 'Flaming Ark is flaming right—', who had in turn reported it to the First Lieutenant, who had only enquired hopefully whether it was large enough to devour the fecund Hyacinthe and then reported it in turn to the Captain, who had instructed the Officer of the Watch to enter it in the ship's log. Finally SBA MacLean had volunteered to assume responsibility. So, officially at least, one dog had been processed through all the proper channels, and was now on the ship's strength.

Even if he had understood, this knowledge would have been little consolation in his present insensate terror. *Tertian* went about her ordained way, her crew long-conditioned and balanced to the cramped discomfort and ceaseless sawing movement of a destroyer slicing through the Atlantic swell. Up on the bridge, Barkis relaxed on a bunk in the Captain's sea-cabin or rolled nonchalantly along the decks in wide-spread nautical gait, conforming effortlessly to the ship's every movement. Below decks in No. 2 mess, Hyacinthe slept the hours away in her small swaying hammock, peacefully unmoved by all uncouth human disturbance.

But to the small newcomer, straining to keep his balance, even his faculties, under a fixed table in a small cramped mess, what was routine to them must have been a heaving nightmare of confusion and terror from the moment he had staggered to his feet in the slippery pitching blackness of the store room.

He had lived his entire life on the open road, yet safely contained within the small nomadic world of which he was the beloved and valued centre. In one flame-seared moment that

66

world had gone, and with it all security: he had come through the terrors of fire and water to waken now in what was possibly the most terrible element of all to him – confinement. Confinement in an unstable, unyielding steel box filled with the hurrying boots of strangers and their unrecognisable speech sounds; his ears assailed by fearful incessant noise, ranging from the routine background of bells and wailing pipes and disembodied voices of the loud hailers, the whine of turbines to the wind's eerie descant, the crashing roar of heavy seas, the thunder of guns that reverberated throughout every inch, and the great muffled shudder of exploding depth charges. An inhuman metallic world now that sought to deafen him to the gentle familiarity of tinkling bells and the clap of hands, the creak of rolling wheels, the notes of birdsong and flute; an arid world that would deaden his senses for ever to the smell of damp woods and fresh green fields, hot living smells of fairgrounds, the promise of wood smoke.

Above all, it must have been the loneliest of worlds, with only the slightest association of voice and smell between this human who now ordered his life, MacLean, and that deep, however brief, attachment to the soldier from whom stretched back his only link with his lost world. The soldier had shared that world once, travelled in the caravan and left his imprint on its people – the transference to him had been of the dog's own volition. Later in the terrors of the sea there had grown a close interdependence. Now there was only this unyielding stranger with the competent but impersonal hands, a brusque exclusion in his voice, and unsmiling eyes.

A rope collar had been fashioned for him, not for restraint, for he was too terrified to move anywhere by himself, but to stop him sliding around the deck, and he was kept tied up with only brief forays on the end of a line to where the depth charges were secured over the stern. Here, in an area frequently washed down by following seas, Barkis came to lift his Olympian leg, or squat, while his attendant of the moment stood by with a hygienic bucket of water. Here, to this sterile, salty substitute for trees and fragrant earth, came the trembling newcomer, creeping low, hesitantly testing the deck as though expecting it to give way beneath his paws, or scrabbling desperately for purchase as it heeled, the whites of his eyes supplicating the white-maned restless unknown that filled the horizon beyond the rails. Barkis displayed an overwhelmingly generous interest when they met there, but the exuberance of his greeting, the excited lash of his whip-like tail and the playful butting of his rock-hard head invariably capsized the small dog's already precarious balance and terrified him even more.

Hyacinthe had appraised him the first day with a cold green gooseberry eye, apparently found nothing to alarm or disquiet, and thereafter ignored him.

Although his body shivered constantly, he was otherwise unanimated. All the spark had gone out of him, the endearing top-knot had been cut off, his ears trimmed short: he was drearily unattractive in his misery, and he had become very thin. He spent the hours routinely in the dark obscurity of the kneehole under the sick bay desk, or under the Mess table, never curled up or sprawled in canine relaxation, but always tensely crouched, giving the impression that he was somehow clinging on against a suspended movement and dared not let go.

Both from safeguard and training, he had been taught never to eat anything offered by strangers. Only one familiar hand had slipped titbits into his expectant mouth, and then always in reward, the same hand that had never touched him save in praise or affection. There had been no unsteady isolated bowl set before him, its unrecognisable contents to be eaten alone or apart. Food had always meant a shared savoury intimacy at the end of the day's work or travel, her plate or the pot to lick clean afterwards, perhaps a morsel fallen from the old man's fingers, a handout from the monkey – and, if there were any doubts over the rights, there had always been her smiling nod of reassurance.

MacLean attributed the dog's refusal of food now to a combination of seasickness and changed environment. In charge of an animal experimental laboratory before the war, he had known plenty of sick and miserable animals in his time to refuse food, and almost always they had become reconciled to their lot in the end and had started eating once more. But as the days passed, and his charge continued to exist on tinned milk alone, he was forced to admit that there was a difference between those withdrawn, hunger-striking animals and this miserable but adamant little dog who would accept a biscuit, then lay it on the deck, where it would remain untouched; or if confronted with a bowl, would give the contents a perfunctory sniff, then turn away as though he had no stomach for them.

MacLean tried seasick remedies, put sulphur in the dog's drinking water; he mixed conditioning powders and emptied them down the unprotesting throat, vitamin pills by the handful followed. He doused the coat with flea powder and searched his memory for every last veterinary remedy dispensed to distraught owners of small pampered dogs who had gone off their food. He even – and this went very much against his principles – tried feeding by hand; but his disapproval could not help but be communicated through his fingers and voice, and in the end it was only by holding the muzzle and waiting until the throat was forced to swallow that he achieved anything, and then the dog retched up again. This behaviour, and the dog's utter dejection and constant shivering irritated MacLean exceedingly: it went against his professional grain. For the first time in his life, he had encountered an animal whose will to resist him was unyielding.

He even consulted the doctor, who thought that the dog might still be shocked, suffering from exposure, inhaled some oil ... at least he was drinking, it couldn't be rabies ... give him time, he'd never heard of a dog starving itself to death.

'My prescription would be time,' he ended, looking sympathetically at the abject huddle with the round baffled eyes at MacLean's feet. 'Time – and lots of TLC.'

'TLC?'

'Tender Loving Care – plus, plus,' said the doctor, who took a perverse delight in rousing his dour SBA's invariable reaction to any sentiment. He was not disappointed now.

'Thank you, sir,' said MacLean, his voice as acidly disapproving as his face.

'Patient's name, rank, and number?' asked the doctor, happily adding a row of hearts and hieroglyphics to 'TLC' on a medical form.

'It hasn't got a name,' said MacLean, stiff with outrage at this foolishness.

The doctor looked up in genuine astonishment. 'Well, you might start in right there with the treatment – at least give it a personality, poor little devil,' he said. 'I wouldn't feel like eating myself if I were nothing but an It,' he added, half to himself, as MacLean departed. And he wondered, not for the first time, at the complex nature of this man whose hands he had seen at work on a tiny sick monkey with the most expert deftness – yet with less actual involvement with his subject than he had seen in a mechanic dealing with a choked carburettor. It was the same with 'It': how, out of the whole ship's company, one who quite obviously had no affinity for dogs should have taken over this one was a corresponding puzzle.

His SBA was a reticent man, and apart from once prying out the fact that he had worked for a vet and in an animal laboratory before joining up at the outbreak of war, the doctor knew little of him other than what he had observed. He spent his off-duty time in the sick bay, when it was empty, reading and knitting or playing solitary chess. Very much a loner, not liked by his shipmates, yet not disliked either – rather one who was treated with wary circumspection, for he more than made up for his small stature by the bite and lash of his tongue. He ran the sick bay and dispensary with impersonal extreme efficiency. The long-mouthed lead swinger got short and scornful shift, but he could show deepest concern and unsparing gentleness towards the wounded or seriously ill. In the six months that he had been on board, the doctor could not fault him in any of his duties.

Periodically after a shore leave, he would appear so drunk at the end of the prow that it was so far only by a miracle – or by a deliberate Nelson-eye approach to his problem on the part of the duty personnel – that he had avoided the defaulters' list. But no matter how monumental the hangover, how green his face, how black an eye, he had never failed to report for duty dead on time in total efficient control of himself, and smelling strongly of peppermints.

'I'm chust partial to a wee dram at times. It helps,' had been his only explanation when the exasperated MO, putting a stitch in above an eyebrow, had asked him once why he had to drink to such heroic excess each time.

'Helps what?' he had persisted.

'To pass the time,' said MacLean woodenly.

The doctor returned to his job of censoring the crew's letters. Over the months he had become expert at skimming over the contents, long familiar with those incautious hands that invariably needed his deleting attention. Among this week's batch was one that he read twice:

HMS TERTIAN
c/o GPO
July 1st 1940

Dear Corporal Sinclair,

It is my sincere hope that when this reaches you, you will be well on the road to recovery. Perhaps even enjoying some sick leave. I write this line just to tell you that I have your belongings in safe keeping. I found the enclosed souvenir among them and enclose it for luck. The clapper was missing, but I have fashioned another.

I would be glad to receive a line from you. There seems

little likelihood that I will be able to despatch the above mentioned article for some time as we are kept on the hop just now. But I will see to it that it reaches you in good condition one day as promised.

Yours sincerely,
Neil MacLean, SBA

It was the first letter of MacLean's that the doctor ever remembered. He had a more retentive memory for names than the writer had credited him with. '*Very* interesting,' he said to himself, wielding the censor stamp, and immensely tempted to write 'and bow-wow to you too!' under its imprint, 'Very interesting but *why*...' He replaced a tiny brightly polished silver bell, neatly cocooned in a pill box.

MacLean wasted no deep thought in a name. He had been brought up on a farm where each succeeding sheep dog had inherited the name of its predecessor. Thus there was always a Ria if it were a dog, and a Meg if it were a bitch. This was therefore a Ria. It was as simple as that.

'I would be obliged if you would be calling the dog Ria to accustom it,' he said to Reid and his messmates over tea, before picking up his book and preparing to read as usual right through the meal. 'Ree-ah,' he emphasized.

'Ria,' said Reid obligingly, 'Ria, *Ria*—' and he leaned over to pat the dog. 'Good dog, *Ria*,' then, 'Eh, but you're nowt but skin and bone, luv – we'll have to feed you up.' At the concern in this voice, the ears pricked slightly and the tail stirred. Reid cleaned his plate with a piece of bread, but his offering was forestalled.

'The dog is getting fed once a day – by *me*,' said MacLean with cold flat emphasis, and returned his eyes to the pages of *Admiral the Lord Nelson*.

So, phoenix-like, and most sadly, arose from the ashes of his former life this new dog, Ria; as unlike that other as it was possible to be: no hint of the vivacious little professional in this stricken-eyed cowering shadow. The only hint of his exceptional intelligence might have been remarked in the short time it took him to put meaning to words of a new language, and to interpret the message of ship's bells and pipes. But in a mess where there was a constant turnover as the watches changed there was little time or opportunity to observe anything as intangible as this. His bewilderment and pathos had reached out to the men as a whole; they had tried to give him the reassurance he so obviously needed, to make him one of them, but their attempts wilted under the consistently disapproving glare of one who so forbiddingly kept himself to himself, and made it quite clear that this extended to his belongings as well.

The stolid Reid, the only man who ever said what he felt like to MacLean, argued the necessity of rigid discipline. 'It's a dog's life all right, the way you're going about it,' he said, and received the not unreasonable reply that an undisciplined animal roaming around underfoot in an emergency could be a real menace.

'It is essential that he learns a set place at all times,' said MacLean, 'and is never distracted from it.'

Reid's reply was succinctly monosyllabic.

In the meantime Ria existed, physically at least, as a fairly adequate diet was being added to the milk in the guise of porridge, gravy and cod liver oil, all of which he lapped up with tidy disinterest.

In contrast, shipboard life held the warmest and happiest of worlds for the monkey, who had no complexities of devotion to suffer a sea change, and almost immediately had become a very distinct personality, with a name, Louis, the beginnings of a wardrobe and some fifteen willing subjects in his personal kingdom of Number Five Mess.

Leading Seaman Lessing, who had owned a capuchin monkey in civilian life, had interested himself in Louis' welfare from the beginning when he had been housed, a sick, listless bundle in a cardboard box in one of the boiler rooms. Here he had received the best clinical attention from MacLean, but grew daily more apathetic. Lessing had insisted that if the little animal did not have some constant contact with a living being he would simply pine away, no matter how excellent the treatment.

After trying, and failing, to persuade Hyacinthe to share the warmth of her fur coat, he took matters into his own hands one day and removed the monkey to the mess deck. Here he provided both warmth and contact with his own body, first wrapping Louis in the folds of a woollen scarf. He slept with this bundle and ate with it on his lap. At the end of his four hours off, when the watches changed, he virtually press-ganged his opposite number into continuing this treatment. For days, Louis was never out of someone's arms or stuffed inside the comforting warmth of a jersey or duffle coat, and by the time it was decreed that he was fit enough to be left to his own devices on the deck for a while, he was everyone's concern.

A seaboot stocking had been cut and neatly tailored to make a pullover; he already owned one pair of knitted shorts with a second pair on the needles; and another pair of devoted hands had netted a small hammock like Hyacinthe's. It was found impossible to train him to the use of Hyacinthe's sandbox however: Louis had a happy disregard for such niceties of behaviour. Fortunately there was no shortage of cotton waste from the engine room, and his shorts were lined with this.

It was an incredibly cramped and congested kingdom, directly above a magazine, much of it already taken up with a maze of pipes and cables, the bolted-down benches and mess tables, lockers, hatches, ladders, even the large round bulk of a gun mounting and ammunition hoists. Yet in it some fifty men, divided between the port and starboard watches, lived, slept and had their comfortless being. At night when the hammocks were slung there were seldom enough to go round and the luckless stretched out on lockers or mess tables. They were seldom dry; the deckhead dripped constantly from con-

74

densation, and in heavy weather some of the water swirling along the decks inevitably found its way down the ammunition hoist and sloshed to and fro to the ship's roll so that even their kit in the lockers was soaked. A rich fug compounded of steaming wool, bilge water, socks, tobacco and the stale reminder of the last meal permeated everything. It was hardly anyone else's idea of the perfect kingdom, but Louis thrived there. From the point of view of a very small monkey it could not have been more ideal, for there was always company, always something going on, always some human only too glad to alleviate the monotony or shut off the mind to the discomfort in the parenthetical company of something so responsive, so innocently amusing and mischievous as a capuchin monkey.

Even when the ship was at action stations and Louis was tethered by a collar and chain to a table, he was still not alone, for there were always two hands stationed at the ammunition whips leading up from the magazine. If nothing was happening he would occupy himself endlessly polishing the table with a much-prized yellow duster in one hand, an empty tin of polish in the other, or swinging in his hammock slung below the table. At the first explosion of guns or depth charges, however, he hopped into the hammock and covered his head in the folds of a long woollen scarf. He was always nervous and particularly mischievous after such a time, and the hands soon learned to keep anything they valued out of his reach afterwards: someone would usually give him an additional cigarette to his daily ration of two as a consoling distraction.

He escaped once, unfortunately fetching up in the Chief Petty Officer's Mess. Here he rifled the drawers, found a tin of Brilliantine, then using a clean shirt as a polishing rag, he stickily burnished everything within reach, including a photograph of somebody's wife and twin daughters. The official reprimand and warning that followed this escapade was so sharp that thereafter Number Five Mess took steps to train their Louis to such a remarkable degree of invisibility when authority was in the offing that it became a nightly challenge to the duty officer making rounds to try and spot him.

Louis' escapade was soon forgotten. Authority, recognising the tedium and discomfort of the lower decks, was benevolent. Perhaps even a little envious, for sometimes the MO, on the professional pretext that he liked to follow up his patients, would borrow Louis for a visit to the wardroom. On the first occasion that he met the Captain there, also visiting, with Barkis as usual in tow, his flaming beard so excited Louis' grooming instincts that he threw a very human tantrum when the time came to return him. Barkis had viewed him with considerable reserve, his pink-rimmed piggy eyes rolling in acute embarrassment: being bidden to suffer without action the indignity of having his tail tweaked by a monkey was too much. Thereafter he tucked it well under and remained firmly seated when he encountered Louis.

Tertian had returned to the Biscay coast after Falmouth and ferried back hundreds more Polish and British troops. Shortly after this she proceeded to Gourock, and there she was taken from the Home Fleet and given over to Atlantic convoy escort duty. The unremitting exhausting grind of those first few hundred miles outward bound to Halifax on the Western Approaches passages were soon intensified when the long-range Focke Wulf Kondors were able to operate out of Bordeaux, and not only attack but act as aerial spotters for U-boats. Although the hands could fall out at action stations if there was no imminent urgency they had to be ready to fall in again at minutes notice, so there was seldom any letting up, and never more than a brief snatch of sleep. But the U-boats were not yet ranging right across the Atlantic, and there was an area, like Tom Tiddler's Ground, before the convoys reached their eighteenth west meridian rendezvous and there dispersed to continue alone or with Canadian-based protection, and *Tertian* turned back with the homeward-bound convoy. Before she steamed back into range of the hungry U-boat packs, there could be a brief interlude when a man might sleep for a few uninterrupted hours, finish a hot meal, or even find a pair of dry socks; a time to obliterate from the mind the shocking toll of lives and tonnage in their last flock and appraise the new assortment.

There might even be time then for the off-duty watch in Number Five Mess to bring out a harmonica or a concertina and entertain – and be entertained by – their mascot.

The moment any music started Louis would jump down from whatever shoulder he was favouring at the moment, bob up and down until someone found his enamel mug, then break into a kind of shuffling dance, skilfully catching anything thrown to him in the mug, gibbering in the grimace that his audience had learned to interpret as a smile. Or, if someone produced the trapeze that needless to say had been fashioned for him, he would go through an expert and unvarying routine of gymnastics. He expected applause, and when he got it would make the rounds with his mug for reward. Sometimes the men teased him by withholding the applause; then he would chatter in frustration, pulling at Lessing's hands, or retire to his hammock and sulk with his back turned, his little blue pullover pulled up over his face. When the claps and whistles were forthcoming at last, he would wait like some temperamental prima donna for the right pitch of rising enthusiasm before he appeared again. When he was really offended – and he was unexpectedly sensitive – it was a long time before the offender could win himself back into favour.

If Louis' gamin, chimerical qualities were a relaxing diversion to tired tense men, then they in turn gave him everything that he could have wished for: the love and constant company that he craved, adulation, warmth and comfort, ingenious toys for his amusement. He even had his own place at the table where he downed thick cocoa or very sweet tea from his own mug, and picked at whatever delicacies the messman

77

and his messmates could heap upon his plate. If he lacked one thing in his little kingdom of Number Five Mess, that was the other half of his life's act, his steed and companion, the dog.

6

It had never been MacLean's intention that dog and monkey should meet – if for no other reason than that the monkey had been from the start totally excluded from the tidy compartment in his mind reserved for the sole responsibility and welfare of dog, small, grey, one; Sinclair, Corporal RASC, property of. Anyway Sinclair had never mentioned the monkey: he must have thought it was dead.

But he had not reckoned on the compartment being invaded by Ria's nose – or by the escaping steam from a fractured pipe in the engine room. One day he returned to the sick bay after treating the monkey for a minor skin ailment. He laid his jacket over the chair, then turned to wash his hands. Under the desk, Ria stirred into sudden life as one of the sleeves hung before his nose. He sniffed intently, his stumpy tail quivered and one ear went straight up. His nose must have given him the certain message that somewhere in this steel maze was hidden another living part of him. Something of purpose or substance must have returned to him then with the message – as though a pin point of light had been glimpsed at the end of a long dark tunnel. There must come a time when his nose must surely lead him to it. . . .

Then, a few days later, a stoker was admitted to the sick bay, seriously scalded and in great pain. *Tertian* was in mid-Atlantic, still within U-boat range, the sole destroyer escort to a convoy under attack most of the way, constantly zigzagging in evasion, sometimes turning hunter herself to shudder to the explosive pattern of her depth charges. In such conditions, with a drip running into his arm, the stoker needed almost constant attention. For the next five or six days Mac-Lean took what sleep he could on a chair by the sick bay cot, appearing only briefly to snatch a meal in the mess, where Reid had undertaken the charge of Ria.

The first evening, spelled off for supper by the doctor, he had returned to find Reid asleep, Ria wedged in at his back, his ears laid back in dog guilt: he had once before attempted to gain the dry security of a bunk, and had been told off then. 'Get down, you,' said MacLean sharply now, and he jumped down at once to the heeling slippery deck. A locker door burst open to a particularly violent lurch and he slid down the deck engulfed in its contents, yelping as he cannoned off the bulkhead. As the deck came up again he started back, whimpering and favouring one paw, but this time MacLean halted him with an outstretched foot. He examined the paw, and Ria licked his hand. He wiped it in irritable disgust.

'Put him back where he was, Doc,' said Reid, his eyes still closed. 'He's not a bloody limpet, and when I'm looking out for him, he stays bloody here in this bunk.' His voice was sleepy and as equable as ever, but there was no mistaking an overtone of clear finality. There was no option: MacLean dropped Ria back on the blanket with ill grace.

'It's no place for a dog,' he said, and picking up a pair of boots he threw one with a noisy clatter back into the locker. 'It will just be the encouragement of bad habits.' He punctuated his words with the second boot.

Reid opened his eyes and smiled up at him. 'Why don't you frick off – and *quietly*, there's a good soul,' he said gently. 'We need our sleep—' He pulled the blanket over his face. Ria's apprehensive eyes peered over his back – then disappeared quickly before the look they received.

MacLean swallowed his warmed-up food, gulped a mug of tea, and returned to his patient. His face was compassionate, his voice comforting, his hands tender as he adjusted the protective cocoon around the man's raw body.

Back in the mess Reid lay awake for a minute or two, one hand absently fondling the dog's ear, then he huddled down under the blanket again, falling asleep almost instantly. Curled up to his back, Ria closed his eyes, heaved a long relaxed sigh of utter content, snuggled closer, then slept too.

Perhaps because of the warm security of this first contact, and the interest and cameraderie that came his way in the following days now that the mess was free of MacLean's disapproving eye, perhaps because he now had a purpose, Ria's confidence gradually returned.

First, and most important, he found his sea legs. Up until now, he had had to be carried up and down ladders. Reid, after much encouragement, placing his paws one after another on the rungs, had persuaded him to scramble up, but the descent was obviously terrifying. Reid stood at the bottom, enticing, the others in the mess encouraged, and Ria crouched at the top, trying again and again to bring himself to make the attempt. Suddenly he launched himself, not down the ladder but into mid-air, straight at Reid who fortunately caught him. The watchers stamped their feet and clapped. His delight in his triumph was touching: his tail quivered to a near wag, and when he was patted and praised and put down he flew effortlessly up the ladder again and prepared for another descent.

'Ooplah, my beauty,' said Reid, his hands out, and down came Ria again, patently delighted with himself. He had performed, and he had been applauded again at last. But this time his reward was his own achievement and Reid's evident pleasure. He soon learned to come down using all four paws, head foremost, but if exhorted by a cry of 'Ooplah' from someone at the bottom he would always launch into midspace.

His next step forward was to show some initiative, and this followed very quickly in a remarkable adaptation. It was hot and crowded in the mess and he was thirsty. For a while he panted unnoticed on a bunk while the men sat around the table over tea. Suddenly he jumped down and stood on his hind legs beside them, balancing easily now to the ship's movement, even walking around the end of the table. He was so obviously asking for something, his eyes intent on each in turn, that a crust was tossed his way. He ignored it, panting, and comprehension dawned; someone fetched a mug of water.

He drained it, then jumped back on the bunk, to lick and groom his paws, a very satisfied little dog of some substance at last, taking in everything around him with round bright eyes, basking in the attention accorded him by this friendly audience.

Fear and the ladder had imprisoned him in the mess before. Now one barrier was down, and he overcame the other next day. He climbed the ladder many times, staying at the top to survey the passing world and assay its scents for longer and longer intervals. Many hands reached down to pat him, and his nose investigated each, some with great interest, and one in particular filled with such promise that he was emboldened enough to trail its owner's boots, until they disappeared up another ladder. He returned to his post, restless and excited. He descended to the mess and whined insistently, only quietening when a would-be sleeper threw a paperback at him in exasperation.

Far from quelling him, this seemed to have a decisive effect; in the comparative quiet of the middle watch he set off on his quest, hesitantly nervous as he gained the top of the ladder, with laid-back fearful ears and belly crouched low, then with increasing upright courage. He had traversed the route to the stern often enough, but never by himself, and always secure at the end of a line. He followed that route now, with many pauses while his quivering nostrils translated the messages wafted from ventilator shafts, door grilles and hatches.

Sunlight streamed in through an opened doorway; he rested his muzzle on the high warm sill and snuffed the wind, until approaching footsteps drove him to retreat into unknown territory. He went on, each forepaw raised and held in turn, step by wary step, tail between his legs, looking back frequently but always urged on by his nose.

He crept past the whining terrors of an open engine room hatch, then wrenched away in panic from a pair of hands that suddenly reached out to him from the hot blast of the gleaming depths far below.

His driving need lent him courage as he flitted up and down companionways and ladders, and along passageways, his coat merging into the grey of steel as he pressed close to the sides, hastening now to a growing certainty; and then down the final ladder, and his eyes could take over at last from his nostrils . . .

He crouched there for a moment, unobserved, his heart beating wildly, searching through the blue haze of tobacco smoke. A terrible journey, but at the end of it he had found a part of his lost self again – there, perched on a man's shoulder, eating a potato, was his monkey . . .

Lessing, sitting at the far end of the mess with his back turned to the ladder, thought for a moment that Louis had gone mad when the monkey had suddenly jumped from his shoulder, squeaking and chattering as never before. He swung now from the overhead pipes then leaped from a hammock to another shoulder, from shoulder to table, where he rammed his potato into a sailor's open mouth in passing, then somersaulted off on to the deck where he scuttled down the length of the mess.

Now Lessing saw the cause of the excitement – MacLean's dog, balanced half way down the ladder, swaying to the ship's roll. Louis leaped for him, yet somehow the dog managed to retain his balance before slithering down the rest of the way. As he gained the deck, Louis now clasped tightly around his neck, the ship rolled heavily and they skidded down the slope coming to rest against the hammock rack from which Hyacinthe had been surveying the vulgar human world before her. Hyacinthe exploded off the pile. Louis reached out a lightning paw and grabbed her tail; she turned – it seemed even in mid-air – and raked his forearm so that he squeaked in pain, whereupon the dog went for her. The deck rose again, and the yipping, squeaking, spitting tangle of mixed fur skidded back and forth and finished up under the table where Lessing doused the uproar with a mug of water.

It was a spectacular first entrance, and received the applause it deserved. Hyacinthe stalked off to soothe her ruffled fur and dignity in the galley. Lessing dried the whimpering Louis, and Ria solicitously licked the scratch. The end of his tail quivered like a tuning fork, and every inch of him was vibrant and eager. Ria had come to full vivid life once more.

Now this monkey haven was where he wanted to be too, and in the remaining days of freedom he would make his way to it whenever possible. Reid was well aware of what was going on, but as Ria was always punctiliously returned by Lessing or one of his messmates in due course after a visit, by unspoken agreement nothing was ever said, and MacLean remained in ignorance of his charge's double life.

Up to now the only brief glimpses that the lower deck had had of this new dog was of a small shrinking shadow at the end of a line on his way to the stern, or a limp shaggy bundle under MacLean's arm. Now a bright-eyed eager little dog would appear, leaping down the ladder to be greeted with an enthusiastic welcome in general and with rapturous affection by Louis.

He was unfailingly patient, even when Louis was at his most mischievous, and would tolerate all liberties, lying still for as long as his tormentor wanted to groom him, jump over or up and down on him, lean against him or hang around his neck; and seemingly only amused if a bowl of water was emptied over him. However, invariably there came a point when Louis became extremely frustrated over his non-co-operation in an act. But, while their performance together had been a way of life to Ria, it had been conditioned by training, and his reflexes must have been too deeply rooted to overcome without commands or signals.

Louis had no such inhibitions, for most of his part of a performance had been built around what he, Louis, liked to do naturally, and when this culminated in a few puffs of a cigarette or some other treat, then he liked to do it even more; the dog was not only his refuge and playmate, he was also the vehicle towards the attainment of that pleasure.

He would perch on Ria's back, leaning low and forward like a jockey tensed for the start, but the start, maddeningly, never came; with encouraging clicks he would jump up and down to urge his mount on. 'Come on, Ria, they're *off*!' the watchers would shout helpfully, but Ria could only sit there with head thrown back and forepaws close together, tensed and ready as he waited for the starting signal that never came. This behaviour so puzzled and irritated Louis that he would jump down and even attempt to drag his partner forward by the collar, but the harder he pulled, chattering in frustration, the more firmly Ria planted his hind-quarters and rolled his eyes beseechingly. To their audience this miniature tug of war was a hilarious act, and was always cheered on. 'Haul away there, Louis,' roared his many supporters, and 'Pull, *pull*—' shouted the Ria few. As Louis could only be appeased by some delicacy he soon learned to turn his frustrations into yet another turn in his repertoire.

Inevitably Ria was offered food and invariably it was refused – until the day he happened to arrive during a meal. Louis was guddling around in his own mess tin, picking out the choicest parts first as usual, and as Lessing watched he picked out a morsel that did not seem to meet with his approval, for he lobbed it over to the dog. It was caught and swallowed in a flash, and Ria moved closer, wagging his tail, his ears cocked expectantly. He was not disappointed: so engrossed in his plate that he did not bother to look up, Louis held out his paw with another reject, and Ria took it gently from his fingers. When Louis had finished, he moved in and polished the mess tin clean. Lessing gave him some of his own dinner and that disappeared too.

Unaware that this was the first solid food that the dog had eaten, his appetite seemed only natural to Lessing. Not only had the crew of the whaler seen them together in the water, but there could be no doubt from their behaviour that these two animals had belonged together formerly, and what more natural than that they should have shared a feeding time. But he was astute enough to recognise afterwards that Ria would never eat unless he, Lessing, were having his own meal at the same time; also that in some uncannily perceptive way the dog seemed to have grasped the complex system of watch keeping and after one mistiming never again appeared in his absence.

But the day came all too soon when *Tertian* made her rendezvous at eighteen degrees west. There she refuelled and turned back with an infinitely more vital flock, laden to its limits with fuel, machinery, tools, food and equipment, a rich prey for the U-boats on the homebound passage.

And there Ria's freedom ended, for shortly after his patient was transferred, clattering down the ladder in an explosive mixture of anger and anxiety came MacLean, haunted every inch of the way in his search from the empty mess by thoughts of his charge being swept overboard, fallen down the engine room hatch, being found in – perhaps even desecrating – off limits territory, penetrating the wardroom ... It was an infuriating anticlimax to find this domestic idyll: Ria, a look of almost besotted pleasure on his face, being very thoroughly groomed by the monkey, the centre of a watching ring as absorbed as Louis himself.

MacLean's relief turned sour at the sight. He called twice but, beyond laying his ears back almost apologetically, Ria did not stir. He strode over and picked up the dog, but Louis hung on determinedly. As fast as he disengaged one paw with his free hand the other curled fast on the collar. He put Ria down on the deck to free both hands: still clutching with one hand, grimacing in fury, Louis made towards this interfering human antagonist the most obscene of his considerable

86

repertoire of obscene gestures. There was a titter of restrained laughter. MacLean, scarlet-faced, tried again to pry the fingers loose, but Louis swung himself on to the dog's back and clung like some small determined Old Man of the Sea.

Lessing took pity and came to help. 'Leave him till the watches change,' he suggested as he disengaged paws. 'Louis always lets him go then without any fuss,' and as MacLean's mouth remained closed like a rat trap, 'I'll bring him back myself—' he added hopefully.

'The dog has no business to be here, now or anytime. Come, you—' said MacLean dismissively, and turned to go. His reluctant shadow fell in at his heels only after being dragged the first few feet.

'Come on, Doc, be a sport—' wheedled the rest of Number Five Mess, faced with the prospect of this new diversion for their spoiled and only child disappearing out of his grasp, 'Give them a treat – poor little orphans, they don't get many—'

For a second, MacLean hesitated. He was exhausted, and he wanted only to get his head down for a few hours' oblivion, freed from all responsibility or worry. But in that moment of indecision, Louis struggled free and scampered across to hang on to Ria's tail, so endearingly comical in his too-long shorts and white rollneck jersey as he tried to drag his companion back that a roar of laughter went up, increasing as the tail wagged furiously so that the tiny body at the end of it quivered in rhythm and the shorts dropped lower and lower. Then as though to complete the burlesque they dropped down altogether, Louis trying to pull them up and out of the way with one hand as he held on grimly to the tail with the other.

'I'll thank you to get yon brute of a monkey off – the now,' said MacLean to Lessing.

Lessing's amusement was stopped cold at the venom in the tone. He shrugged and pried the furiously protesting

87

Louis loose. He made one last attempt. 'But why *not* let them be together when they can? He's sort of settled down here with Louis, and he's no trouble. Why don't you give it a try anyway?'

'The dog's settled – with *me*,' said MacLean. '*I'm* responsible, and I'll not have any daft to-ing and fro-ing all over this ship – free to make a nuisance of itself where it shouldn't be,' he added with a meaningful scowl at Louis as he picked up Ria and left.

'Bastard!' summed up Number Five Mess when he was safely out of earshot – a man never knew that he might not have to report sick one day – and turned to consoling their Louis. 'Who the 'ell does he think he is, 'Itler?' inquired a solo indignant voice. 'Fricking little tyrant, that's wot.'

When he reached the upper deck, MacLean put Ria down and went out into the fresh darkness, making his way aft. He leaned over the guardrail, now watching the straight white path of the wake rolled out behind as the *Tertian* slipped through a calm blackness, now watching the small blur that was Ria investigating the bases of the depth charge mountings for traces of Barkis.

The destroyer steamed steadily on the starboard flank of the convoy, her whole length tuned this night to a contentment of seagoing sounds, the sibilant swish of water against the hull soothing the low constant moaning of the funnel. But the sea held no siren sounds for MacLean; he hated it at the best of times, and for the moment he was deaf to everything except the laughter still ringing in his ears. He bitterly regretted his quixotic promise, and all the subsequent complications of fulfilment, the baffling resistance of the dog. He found himself resenting now the forfeiture of precious off-duty time that could be better spent in considering chess problems or getting on with a book; above all, the disquieting intrusion into the ordered fastnesses of his mind. His thoughts churned over the humiliating episode with the monkey as steadily as the ship's screws, the wake of his frustrations rolling out as lengthily over the bleakness of his heart.

A dark figure detached itself from the darker mass of the after superstructure, and a soft whistle followed. It was the Leading Telegraphist, tonight one of the depth charge party, with another two hours of his watch to go and glad of any distraction. Ria went to him and cheerful sounds of greeting followed. MacLean had moved near enough to see that Ria was *standing on his hind legs offering a forepaw*. Before so offensive a spectacle, there was nothing that Mac-Lean wanted to do more in the world at that moment than to heave both overboard and set off one of the depth charges over them.

'How's things, Doc?' inquired the voice amiably.

'Fine, fine, chust *fine*...' snarled MacLean, his face now six inches away from the startled Telegraphist, and to an explosive *'Come!'* that brought Ria slinking to his heels, he turned abruptly and vanished through the hatchway. ('Blimey, you could almost smell the sulphur – like the Demon King in the pantomime he was,' said the Telegraphist, regaling his messmates later.)

Back in the sick bay, he filled the kidney basin that now bore the label 'Dog only' with water and set it down before Ria, then shook out the daily ration of vitamin pills into his hand from a bottle. The pills were grimly dropped down Ria's submissive throat; the empty dish carefully washed and put away. He removed his shoes and jacket and turned in on the cot. Ria lay down by the open door. Two minutes later MacLean was asleep. Two hours later, Ria still lay with his head on his paws, his dark eyes wide open and unseeing, as though they were fixed on some point far beyond the immediate boundary of the flat before him – far beyond the bows of the Ark and the endless expanse of ocean, in fact.

7

It would have astonished Neil MacLean, even deeply offended him if he had heard himself described as tyrannical or insensitive, when he was merely discharging his exacting obligation with the utmost conscientiousness.

He came from crofter stock in a thriving west Highland farm, from forebears as at home on the sea in a fishing boat as on the hills. He was the youngest son, the seventh, a sickly asthmatic child, prone to all the allergic ills of his kind, a cossetted, undersized misfit in a family of tall strong brothers, for ever running to catch up, for ever falling behind.

His father was also a seventh son, but despite the portentous mutterings and sidelong glances of the old people of the village, the only singular manifestation that might have been said to set this child apart was the marked reluctance of any domestic or farm animal to be near him. As a strong aroma of Friar's Balsam from the steaming asthma kettle perpetually enveloped him, with pungent overtones of the eucalyptus oil with which his wheezing chest was rubbed, his family did not find this altogether surprising. The same down-to-earth explanation prevailed when, as he grew older, he seemed to be able to subdue or dominate the animals by his presence alone: small wonder that before fierce waves of Vicks Vapour Rub, the most recalcitrant cow, the wildest of dogs, the maddest of bulls seemed to be almost anaesthetised into submission. Altogether it seemed a very sensible, satisfactory explanation as the boy could no more tolerate their presence than they could his, for the closer the proximity or inadvertent contact with an animal and he was seized with the dread wheezing and fighting for breath.

He was sent to a specialist who produced a list of positive allergy tests as long as his mother's face as she listened with polite scepticism to the learned man expounding further on the psychological causes that might underlie the physical symptoms of asthma – maternal rejection, sibling rivalry, and guilt complexes all rolled smoothly off his tongue. Such haverings – and costly ones at that – she had never heard; far from rejecting her youngest son, she had bestowed more affection and attention on him than any of his brothers, rivalry was out of the question as there was a considerable gap in years between him and his next brothers; and as for *guilt* – Neil had been the most docile and obedient little boy, quite unlike his healthily mischievous brothers.

However, the visit did have a productive effect. Shortly afterwards, Neil was sent to the drier climate of inland Morayshire to board with an aunt who owned nothing more potentially disturbing than a budgerigar, and go to school there. The improvement was dramatic: although he was always to remain undersized and thin, he grew out of all allergies. Furthermore, on the east coast, no one cared whether he or his father had six or sixteen brothers. But a residue of his strange power over animals remained, recognised by an astute local vet who took the boy on to help in the school holidays at first, then later as a full-time assistant when he left school.

He became the most efficient handler of animals that the vet had ever experienced, and he selflessly helped and encouraged the young man towards the goal of veterinary college. But after two academically successful years of college, he suddenly quit. He returned to his assistant's job, and the disappointed vet could get nothing more illuminating out of him other than that 'studying and the like was no the life' for him. He returned home only once during this period, and there, having by now almost forgotten its terrors, he had such a traumatic attack of asthma that thereafter he made this the excuse never to return.

He had married eventually. As uninformatively and mysteriously as he did most things, he returned from a holiday on the island of Mull with a soncy red-haired girl, who teased him unmercifully about his pernicketiness – the only one who had ever teased him in his life; and who with all her extrovert flaming haired nature loved him even while she laughed at him, and told him how wonderful he was, so that he became transformed and wonderful in his love for her. Two and a half idyllic years later, on a visit home to her parents in Mull, she was drowned crossing to Iona in her father's fishing boat. Only her father's body was washed up later; the sea kept for ever his Margaret and all that had been their life, and Neil MacLean never again saw the streaming tendrils of the dark red seaweed undulating gently below its surface without thinking of a bright drowned flame.

After the empty mockery of a funeral service, he had given his notice with polite formality to the vet; then, stocked up with whisky, he had returned to their cottage, locked the door and pulled the blinds, answering no neighbourly knock or voices; only seen when he emerged twice a day to feed Margaret's pullets at the bottom of the garden. Her grey cat returned once to cry distractedly outside the door, after which it took to the hills and went wild.

At the end of two weeks he walked out of the cottage, his private wake over. He buried the bottles in the hill behind, and locked the cottage door behind him. He walked away without a backward look, carrying in one hand a small suitcase, and dangling from the other the six plucked carcasses of the pullets. His best suit hung in folds on him, but the trousers had knife-edge creases, his shoes shone brilliantly; his face was freshly shaved and expressionless as stone. The six pullets he gave to their nearest neighbour, returning at the same time a pound of sugar that Margaret had borrowed, so that her kindly face was scarlet with shocked grief. The key he handed over to the vet, receiving in return his letter of the highest recommendation to a colleague, now director of the animal laboratory attached to a famous teaching hospital in London. He then walked to the station, arriving with his ticket on the platform at the precise moment as the south-bound train drew in, and he left Morayshire five minutes later wheezing and struggling for breath as agonisingly as when he first came there as a boy.

It was not long before he became the head attendant in charge of the laboratory animals; and it was not long before the meticulous conditions in which they now lived became a byword among other laboratories. No post-operative patient ever received such undivided professional attention as did the animals in MacLean's care, nor lived so long afterwards, to the gratification of those conducting the experiments. The luckless shaven-haired monkey or rat, guinea pig or dog bent on renouncing the laboratory world for ever found itself opening its eyes on it once more from the antiseptically scrubbed floor of its cage, its drinking vessel freshly charged, its dressings ingeniously barred from investigation, its recovery a command – even, if necessary, its benefactor would minister long hours overtime to make sure it was carried out.

No animal ever bit his ministering hand, no animal cowered away from him; and no animal ever greeted him with pleasure, not even the long-term residents in whom almost every attendant had a friendly involvement which was returned by the animals themselves. His uncanny power, and his dispassionate material involvement could not have found a better outlet. He treated the inmates as machines to be kept in perfect working order. His attitude might seem inhuman to others, but his care was never other than humane; and he would not tolerate any unnecessarily painful or clumsy handling or any form of teasing of the animals from his assistants.

He volunteered the day after war broke out, and it was typical that, hating the sea, he should go straight to a naval recruiting office. He was undersized admittedly, but he was physically A1 classification, and when his veterinary and hospital experience were revealed, the medical officer recommended him for training as a Sick Berth Attendant, and under his pen MacLean, Neil Roderick, D/JX 3427, (Presb.) grew an official inch in height.

This was the rigid complex little man, bitterly inturned, to whom fate had sent a small cherished extrovert of a dog; a man who set his highest stands of admiration by the historical giants of endurance, strength and self control. A slight shivering dog who pranced on his hind legs, and allowed a doll-sized monkey all liberties, who could not even face his food – such a dog would not exactly enhance their heroic image. If he could have admired any dog enough to wish it for his own it would have been one like the great barrel-chested Barkis, that solid mass that stood foursquare and fearless to anything, that invincible muscled missile of the ladders. Certainly not a dog who still winced and shuddered to noise, who seemed to *float* down those ladders, light and graceful as a feather. (He was not to know that Ria could have demonstrated a performing verve on those ladders – such as jumping from rung to rung on hind legs alone – that for strength of muscle and control would have made Barkis' headlong dive seem rudimentary. Fortunately this embarrassing accomplishment was never revealed to MacLean, and by the time Lessing and his messmates discovered it they had learned to hold their peace.)

If he had ever considered their mutual problems, he might have said that, like himself, this dog could not help being small – it could not even help being French, he might have added – but at least it could conform to a more normal dutiful canine mould, with all four feet planted firmly on the ground, and a healthy appetite to boot.

So Ria, who was only what he was, and what his forebears had always been, a dog to amuse and take the minds of men off other things, shivered and was increasingly bewildered by the disapproval and the denial of all that he knew, as MacLean strove daily to overcome the centuries and produce

94

something that approached his idea of what a dog should be – if he were going to be stuck with one.

But the dog's needs, or character, were too strong now to be subject to the man's will. Time and time again, with infinite cunning, when he had learned the times that kept MacLean occupied with his duties, he would judge the moment; always soundless, he seemed to have acquired the ability to suddenly vanish. If tied, he slipped the collar or bit through the line, then straight to the lower deck and the haven of Number Five Mess, no fear or hesitancy now on the way, but a swift confident passage. Invariably he was retrieved, invariably he returned; and no appeal from Lessing or anyone could persuade MacLean to change his mind and permit the visits.

Number Five Mess found his unyielding attitude beyond their total comprehension; if their beloved Louis enjoyed the company of Ria, then it followed that this should be forthcoming, and they could not fathom this refusal to make both parties happy by a similar indulgence with Ria. It became quite an issue. 'The flipping Führer's on his way—' the groan would go around when they saw Ria's ears flick apprehensively, minutes before they heard the footsteps. 'It's back to concentration camp for you, Frogdog.'

Louis, as though aware of his kingdom's disapproval, took an almost human delight in irritating Ria's pursuer. The result was often cruelly humorous as MacLean's face, when he was dourly set on retrieving his errant dog, bore a startling resemblance to the monkey's. The kissing sounds that Louis made when he was feeling affectionate were always soft and gentle; MacLean was invariably greeted with loud and vulgar smacking of lips, or went on his way to the accompaniment of Louis' coarse version of a raspberry.

The strain was beginning to tell. He found himself dreading the trip to the lower deck, and disliking the monkey with a repulsion and animosity that he had never before felt for anyone, let alone singling out an animal for such distinction.

95

Not just for its humiliating behaviour, but for the disturbance to his mind, and the upsetting of routine and control, the distraction of always having to be on the alert to forestall the next vanishing act. His irritation and worry over Ria's lack of appetite increased too, for now this disconcerting animal was beginning to show disinterest in his carefully fortified porridge mix, and seemed to have been living on water alone for the last few days. . . .

Inevitably came the time when he was confronted with the scene of Ria and Louis sharing a mess tin – worse still, the monkey was actually feeding the dog, his delicate little hands guddling around in the tin until they fished out a delicacy which was then tossed into the waiting eager mouth.

'He's right hungry today,' said the innocent Lessing, looking up from his own plate. 'Scoffed his own, and now he's after something from Louis. Meat, potatoes, beans – the lot. Did you know he could sit up and salute? I thought I'd taught him, but he was so quick, I'm certain he knew it all before – just didn't know the English for it, I suppose. He's a sharp one—'

But his last words were directed to MacLean's back; overcome with such a mixture of revulsion and mortification, he had said nothing – but so forcibly that for once Ria leaped with alacrity up the ladder before him and made straight for his proper obscurity under the desk, regardless of the fact that the doctor's feet were already there. He looked very subdued, only too well aware that once again he had offended, and that the offence this time must be unusually grievous.

'You look very guilty, my lad,' said the doctor. 'What have you been up to this time?'

He pressed against these friendly legs as though seeking protection from he knew not what.

But it was Barkis who was to be his saviour of the day. Barkis's claws to be exact, for in the confinement of a destroyer they were not worn down normally, and when they reached the point of curving over his pads they had to be cut. All his wiles and strength went into his resistance to this painless operation; it took three men to hold him down, and a fourth to wield the clippers.

'You're wanted on the bridge,' said the doctor as a set-faced MacLean appeared. (That his charge should occupy the same kneehole as an officer's legs was yet another offence – this time in the unseemly category.) 'Operation Toenails, you lucky chap. I told the Captain that with all your experience, you probably had some magical quick tricks up your sleeve. And God help you if you haven't – I did the job last time and it took me nearly a week to recover.'

'Out you come,' the doctor said when MacLean had gone, and took a sugar lump from a cache in the drawer. Ria emerged and sat expectantly as the sugar was balanced on his nose, then with a professional flip, he sent it high in the air, caught and swallowed it. The next lump was thrown and caught with the same expertise, despite several teasing feints in the opposite direction. 'Clever dog!' said the doctor, and ruffled the silky ears, smiling down with a conspiratorial wink.

MacLean arrived at the day cabin off the bridge to find there the brawny Yeoman to whom Barkis was much attached, and the Captain's steward, Smith. It was a sunny morning, *Tertian* steaming steadily, and the unsuspecting Barkis peacefully asleep on the bridge. The Captain whistled him in, and he came to the door with his powerful rushing roll, paused, sensed his impending doom and backed out hastily.

'Grab him, Yeoman,' shouted the Captain, and the signalman leaped in a flying tackle. Barkis rolled over and waved his paws supplicatingly. Nothing would induce him to get to his feet again; he appeared to be able to ooze out of every attempt to lift him, like a sack of liquid lead.

MacLean, watching this performance and thinking that if he had Barkis to himself for five minutes he would have the claws clipped without further fuss, suggested that the patient be slid or dragged by the collar into the cabin and there hauled on to the chart table for the operation. Barkis had a neck like a tree trunk and could have been hauled for miles without feeling it, but: 'Oh, I don't think Barkis would like *that*,' said the Captain. 'He'd be most unwilling, wouldn't he then, poor boy?' he added tenderly to the inert white bulk, quivering at his feet.

MacLean was horrified; images were toppling off their pedestals all round. He had always respected both dog and man for size and dignity, calm authority, cool courage and discipline – yet one was grovelling on the deck before the completely painless prospect of having his toenails cut, and the other was demoralised with maudlin sympathy.

'Softly, softly, catchee monkee,' said the Captain, and cooing persuasively with promises of chocolate, he managed to lure the trembling bulk on to his bunk and thence on to the chart table. 'Now!' he said suddenly, and like a well-trained team, he, Smith and the Yeoman pounced. Barkis opened his mouth in a dreadful scream and fought like a tiger. MacLean hovered on the outskirts with the clippers waiting to grab a paw; he got one for a second, held on grimly, but only got two claws clipped before Barkis had fought his way to the edge of the table and then on to the floor, where he collapsed on his back again. It was very hot. All wiped their brows and took time out before the next round.

MacLean had never witnessed such a scene in all his life. It was more than he could stand; they could be here the rest of the morning. 'If I might be making a suggestion, sir,' he said at last. 'It is that we knock him out and proceed with the operation while he is unconscious?'

The Captain looked at him in shocked surprise. 'Apart from the fact that it would take a sledge hammer to knock Barkis out,' he said, 'I don't think he would like that.'

'I am not meaning a blow, sir,' said MacLean, his voice becoming more Highland by the moment with embarrassment both at having to stoop to this professional level, and meeting a suddenly defenceless hero upon it at the same time. 'I was thinking that we could knock him out with a wee whiff of something—' He could see the Captain's worried expression, and before there was time to be told that Barkis wouldn't like that either, he hurried on to explain that it was the most merciful way; that the vet always employed it on strong sensitive dogs like Barkis – just a few drops of ether, and clip, clip, and it was all over before the patient realised what had happened. 'And no nasty after-effects,' he added soothingly, almost choking on the words.

Still faintly dubious, the Captain sent for the doctor who agreed, straight-faced and solemn, with MacLean's suggestion. A mask and ether were produced, and peacefully, quietly, and in orderly ship-shape fashion Barkis parted with his excess nails.

Thanking MacLean afterwards, the Captain asked about Ria – he was a fine-looking little dog, he had thought on the few occasions he had seen him. Most intelligent, and – he had been about to say 'amusing', but for some unknown, unconsidered reason he substituted 'and full of guts too' – he would have said.

Astonished that the Captain had even been aware of Ria, taken aback by the obvious sincerity of this praise from a man he admired above all others, MacLean was speechless for a moment. Fine looking? Intelligent? Full of guts? *Ria*?

As he swept the last neat crescents of claw on to a piece of paper, speech returned: 'I had not thought on it, sir,' he said politely, then added with considerably more conviction, 'But, aye, he certainly is a determined wee b...beast.' He turned his attention to Barkis, still lying on the table with a slit of eye open and a silly pleased smile on his thin pink lips. He folded back one of the white ears, then suddenly bent over it so closely that it looked as though he were whispering into its depths.

He straightened up and sniffed disapprovingly. 'Dirty ears,' he said. 'I will be cleaning them out. Come with me, you—' Barkis slid off the table and laid the shameful ears back, a picture of abject apology.

'I will return him in fifteen minutes, sir,' said MacLean straightening smartly to attention before exiting with Barkis rolling obediently along behind, looking almost as bemused as the Captain. Whereas MacLean, for once, looked rather satisfied with himself.

Later that afternoon as he sat at the desk, Ria suddenly came to him and pushed a cold nose into his hand. Reminded of Barkis's unsavoury ears, he lifted one of the softly folded ones under his hand and inspected the delicate spotless convolutions within. Pleased with what he found, he let his hand lie for a moment on Ria's head. 'They'll do,' he said. Ria's tail was delighted at such praise, he grinned, turning his upper lip back over his teeth, and MacLean then inspected the shining teeth as grimly as if he expected to find signs of decay already from the illicit diet of Number Five Mess.

Suddenly he was very conscious of the difference between these jaws and the powerful shark-like ones of Barkis; the fragility of the skull beneath his hand and its almost weightlessness upon his knee; Ria's round vulnerable eyes, Barkis's protected slits. His mind went back to these same teeth gleaming from the black oil-slimed mass of the soldier: this same wee jessie of a dog had then endured over eight hours in the water, and heaven knew what else beforehand – yet still had fight in him. It occurred to him that the mighty Barkis's build would not have stood up to those hours in the water. 'Full of guts,' the Captain had said – maybe he wasn't so far wrong. And intelligent – well, yes, he was no fool. As to 'fine looking' – fine boned certainly, but he stood well nowadays, straight legs – and if he'd keep his head and ears up the way they were now, he wouldn't be so bad looking at that. . . .

'You'll do,' he said almost grudgingly. 'Aye, you'll do.'

Contact with the Captain and Barkis must have been catching; for the second time in his thirty-eight years of life he had spoken words that were neither commands or refusals to an animal, words that assumed the comprehension of human thought. Head to one side, ears cocked, Ria's receptive eyes searched the face above as though expecting something further. But at that moment eight bells sounded, the change of watches; time for his routine inspection of his first aid packs stowed on every gun mounting throughout the ship. He secured Ria by a new length of stronger line and left.

He climbed the ladder to A gun first, and having reached the platform found Ria immediately behind him, the collar slipped. Exasperated, he scowled down, but Ria, ears at a demure half-mast, gazed studiously into the distance. It was too late to return with him now – and at least this time he had not made for Number Five Mess. He continued his rounds, up and down ladders, the dog, cat-footed, close behind, yet never in the way.

They returned to the mess; time now, too, for his meal, and the defeating disinterest of Ria in his – the routine battle. He set the dish down, already more tense than usual, his mouth drawn down as he remembered the intimacy of the monkey's fingers in another dish. Ria gave the unappetising contents his usual perfunctory sniff and turned away. MacLean determinedly edged the bowl towards him again with the toes of his boot, then bent the dog's head over it.

Reid, already eating, watched in silence for a moment, them, 'For Christ's sake, man,' he said in a sudden rare burst of irritation, 'if you'd stop looking as though you had a mouth full of razor blades perhaps the dog would eat something – it's enough to put anyone off their grub!'

MacLean looked up, startled. Then suddenly he smiled, almost shamefacedly. 'Perhaps I am just a thing over-anxious,' he admitted.

'And talk about a dog's dinner –' said Reid, looking down at the bowl in disgust. 'Who'd want to eat that grisly looking muck?' He ladled some of his own plate on to the bowl, stirring it around with a finger.

'Come on, Mam's little luv, eat up your luverly dins-dins,' he said, in such a high falsetto imitation that MacLean could not help laughing – such an unexpected sound that Ria looked at him, his eyes round and astounded.

'Go on – eat up –' said MacLean still laughing, and to his astonishment Ria set to and polished the bowl clean, so obviously ravenous that MacLean gave him some of his own.

From then on there was to be no refusal of meals; a battle had been won. There would have been no doubt in MacLean's mind as to which had triumphed if the point had ever been raised: dogs always came round in the end; he knew. Still, he decided, perhaps Reid had a point – and anyway it could do no real harm to discipline if the dog continued to eat at the same time as himself – and maybe even have something of his own hot dinner. There was nothing more professionally abhorrent than a skinny looking dog. It was interesting, though, that a dog should actually have *preferences* as to where or how it should eat . . . .

Or that anything the merest shade different, the slightest tinge of drama, could assume such colourful importance apparently in the day to day lives of shipboard animals. This was his next discovery when a few days later he watched first Ria and then Hyacinthe shoot out of a hatchway on deck as *Tertian* drew within hailing distance of the last limping ship in the convoy, an elderly rust-stained tramp steamer that had straggled further and further behind all day with engine trouble. They must have received the summons from Barkis on his vantage point of the bridge as he was hurling greetings across the water to a grizzled Aberdeen terrier tucked under the tramp skipper's arm – a small stocky figure on the bridge who, apart from a salt-stained bowler hat, looked not unlike a grizzled old Aberdeen himself. The terrier was yipping hysterically back.

Ria was beside himself with excitement: Hyacinthe had leaped on to the meat safe and had a grand stand seat at all that was going on, but at deck level his view was obscured. He ran up and down, whining, hesitated at the bridge deck ladder, then turned – to MacLean's relief – and scrambled up the fo'c'sle ladder to the platform of A gun. One of the bearded scaramouche crew at the rusty rails heaving up and down before whistled to him and held up a ginger cat, waving its paw in greeting. Ria wriggled and grinned and cavorted precariously in return.

When the exchanges through loud hailers were over – courteous enquiries and exhortations from *Tertian* and decidedly salty disclaimers and asides from the tramp's bridge – the Captain released his silencing grip on Barkis's mouth and put the loud hailer before it. Not to be outdone, the skipper turned his mouthpiece over to his terrier and a dreadful amplified duet ensued. From the gun mounting Ria threw back his head and howled to make a trio of it as *Tertian* moved off again.

MacLean began to take an increasing interest after this in the way that the animals occupied their waking hours, seeing them for the first time not as sick or healthy specimens but as individual personalities. Convoy-watching seemed to hold the most fascination, presumably because of its possibilities of other animal encounters – and he had not realised before that almost every ship carried its quota of assorted mascots – but even a seagull snatching a crust, a bucket rolling down the deck, spray flicking over the rails, held immense potential. In fact, there appeared to be no limits to the apparent human trivia that could be magnified into the most satisfying animal drama.

He found himself more and more absorbed and often amused by the astonishing dimensions opened up through those eyes: Ria's expressive querying ones always on the faces of men, compared to the opportunistic scanning for action of Louis; Barkis's confidently cunning slits across which no shadow of doubt or justification ever flitted; the pure manipulation of her subject in Hyacinthe's stare. And from these observations, came the intriguing revelation that all these separate personalities – with the occasional temperamental exception of Louis – could merge and accommodate each with the other without conflict.

8

The Atlantic convoys were the very life lines of England now; severance would mean a total blockade, so that in the end, even this last defiant little island bastion must surrender – or starve. The responsibility of keeping these lines open, protecting the vital convoys, lay mainly with the destroyers, but in the preceding months twenty-two had been sunk and forty-five damaged, almost half their total strength. What was left – and many of them dating back to 1917 – had to be spread from the north Atlantic to the vulnerable Channel, from the Western Approaches to the Mediterranean, where pressure was mounting daily now that Italy had entered the war. Endlessly protecting, hunting, evading, and fighting-off attack became more and more a test of the limits of human endurance for a destroyer's crew, when all the body cried out for – if it could not be warm and dry – was a few hours of unbroken sleep, and even the most stolid temperament became frayed at the edges.

Two hundred and seventy-four ships were sunk between June and October at a cost of only six U-boats, and now a fleet of superbly equipped fast commerce raiders was in operation. But against all odds, with engines kept going by seeming miracles sometimes, with dirty boilers and straining plates, with exhausted crews, the convoys kept on coming as that desperate summer of 1940 wore on into autumn gales, in the battle for the Atlantic. '*Das glückliches Zeit*', the Happy Time, the German navy called it. The Royal Navy and the

Merchant Service did not have time to call it anything, and if they had, it would have been unprintable.

In these conditions, the most important adaptation a shipboard animal had to learn was the art of keeping out of the way; to be so tuned into urgency and strain that, while the shrill of Action Stations meant instant activity to humans, to them it signalled withdrawal into the most unobtrusive passivity they could find; to enter a state that needed not water nor food, comfort nor company, for there was little chance of receiving any. Barkis secure in his lofty bunk, Louis and Hyacinthe in their hammocks – more often than not curled into a single ball nowadays – they turned themselves off into a kind of temporary hibernation, their bodies sometimes twitching to the thud of underwater explosions, their noses wrinkling to the bitter smell of cordite, but still, it seemed, deeply asleep. Apparently sizing up the situation, Ria never made any attempt to join the monkey at these times, although, paradoxically, he had more opportunity then.

He also had far more close attention and company than usual then, for the doctor – to whose cheerful personality he was devoted and who borrowed him often for company – did not stand regular watches, and apart from routine duties there were many hours when he – and MacLean too, to a lesser extent – were on standby only. These hours could be endlessly tedious, whiled away with books or a growing interest in sketching by the doctor, or a combination of reading and knitting socks by MacLean. Sometimes they could be bleak and harrowing hours: watching the night skies redden to a blazing tanker, the awesome fireworks of an exploding ship, the sickening blank where a living ship had been only a minute before; or, worst of all, the lonely little marker lights flickering on the waves afterwards, the faint cries fading in *Tertian*'s wake. Then inactivity could be almost unbearable. Then the appalled, identifying mind sought distraction in the very normality and unconcern of a dog; a dissociation that was yet an association, for while Ria could have no comprehension of events, he could gauge the human mood and respond accordingly.

On the few – sadly few – occasions when *Tertian* could stop to pick up survivors, or they were transferred from another ship, frozen, shocked men would be crammed into every available space; cabins and flats and wardroom were given over to the wounded, and then only was there the mixed blessing of exhaustion in activity for the doctor and MacLean. And then Ria too went into the same state of suspended animation as the other animals, securely wedged in under the end of a mattress in the mess.

He had become relaxed now in MacLean's company during the enforced sharing of the worst hours of a convoy's struggle for survival, often stretched out in sleep as needles clicked and pages turned, close and companionable. Yet MacLean could not help noticing that he was subtly transformed in another man's presence, and very obviously and enthusiastically transformed if the other happened to be Reid or Lessing or the doctor in particular, or any other members of either mess.

In a deep, dark and hitherto unused corner of his mind, this knowledge nagged. Still, he was rid of his former irritations now; there were no problems over food, no humiliating visits to Number Five Mess, no need to tie Ria – wherever he was left, he was always there on his return (even if, as Mac-Lean now suspected – with a sneaking admiration at the cunning – he had arrived back probably only a few minutes before). All in all, the dog had settled in amazingly well, and had turned out to be no trouble even in the most exigent circumstances.

Which was just as well, he reflected one morning, for it seemed likely that it would be months before he would be free of responsibility. The first mail for weeks had brought a letter from Donald Sinclair's wife. Her husband was now off the dangerously ill list, she reported, but one lung would remain permanently collapsed; he would remain in hospital for some time yet, and would be invalided out of the army in due course:

Then, God willing, one of these fine days we will be able to take the dog off your hands at last. It cannot have been easy for you, looking after him on a boat and all, and Donald has fretted often over what he put upon you when he was not, as he says, himself. For a while he could remember very little, now it is gradually coming back. One day we hope to repay you, even if it is only with our thanks and hopes of friendship. My Aunty knitted the enclosed for you . . .

The enclosed was a pair of socks. MacLean examined them critically. Aunty was an expert, but had been over-generous in length. They would do nicely for Reid.

He put the letter away, his feelings very mixed, and went out into the warm September sunshine on deck. It had been an exciting and eventful time, these last three days, and an almost holiday atmosphere still prevailed in every quarter of *Tertian* as she swung gently to her buoy off the fishing port of Oban.

They had been diverted from the Clyde on the homeward leg and sent on up the west coast of Scotland on a reported sighting of two U-boats. One of the quarry had escaped, but the other was hunted up a long sea loch until trapped and forced to the surface – whereupon she had promptly scuttled. The crew, complete even to a sinister parrot which swore fluently in English, was picked up by a jubilant *Tertian* and taken to the nearest port, Oban, as she was running low on fuel. There she disembarked her not altogether glum captives, and among the congratulatory signals that followed was one delaying their return to the Clyde for twenty-four hours, thus giving both watches some hours ashore.

This was familiar ground to MacLean, the waters all too familiar, and he had hoped never to see them again. The mountainous island of Mull dominated the western horizon, and some twenty miles away as the crow flies north, but nearer eighty by road, was the farm where he had been born. This was the land of his forebears, and of Margaret's. Twenty-four hours here could only be twenty-four deeply disturbing hours too long in his estimation.

It was a Sunday, and in the rare peace of make and mend that settled over the ship after Divisions, he settled himself with his back against the aft superstructure. One watch was going ashore in search of what limited diversion a Highland town on the Sabbath pubs-closed afternoon could offer. Most of the remaining watch slept below, only the few who were not afraid of fresh air sprawled around the deck in the sun, a good stodgy ship's dinner behind them, the prospect of a good stodgy tea ahead with a couple of hours uninterrupted kip in between.

But MacLean was not one to waste the idle hour: he knitted, and as he knitted he read (*General Gordon, Hero of Khartoum*), Ria tidily disposed on one side, a mug of tea on the other.

The gentle rise of mainland hills stretched before him, vividly slashed with bracken's fiery russet and the deep purple of heather. Across the intervening water a light wind carried the peaceful sounds of church bells and sheep bleating – and, to a sensitive interpretive nose, all the exciting, nostalgic and tantalising smells of sunwarmed earth. The only other nose in the ship's company that might have appreciated the wind's promise, Barkis, was already ashore with the Captain, realising them to the full. Ria rose and stood by the rail, his nose twitching, his ears flickering, his eyes searching for the source of this paradise. He whined, and MacLean whistled softly, but Ria did not even turn his head. He whined, more insistently, and only turned back reluctantly to a sharp 'Come *here*!' – but not to lie down, to sit and snuff and quiver. The distraction irritated MacLean, immersed in the most exciting part of General Gordon, 'Wheesht,' he said curtly, standing resolutely on the Residency steps in Khartoum and almost matched in height with the gallant General.

Further along the deck, Lessing appeared with Louis who, in tribute to the sun, wore a sleeveless white singlet instead of his customary pullover. Over this was a shoulder harness to which was attached a long light line. Louis clutched a grey mouse from which he had long ago removed the clockwork insides; crouched on Lessing's shoulder he looked like a small owl with its prey, his eyes as all-seeing. Lessing put him on the deck and settled down to write letters, from time to time patiently removing a grasping paw from his pen or the mouse from his writing pad. Louis wandered further afield and soon, inevitably, he had aroused a devoted slave or two to amuse him.

Ria switched his gaze off the shore and watched, his tail quivering. Beside him MacLean knitted determinedly before advancing hordes of yelling dark-skinned natives.

One of Louis' admirers tossed him a biscuit; he caught it neatly and suddenly scampered along the deck towards Ria. But the line tautened ten feet away and Louis rocked from one foot to another in frustration for a moment, then tossed the biscuit with remarkable accuracy straight at Ria's mouth. Ria's jaws opened, snapped shut, and the biscuit vanished.

MacLean tried to keep his eyes on the print, to ignore the intrusion in Khartoum, but a monkey in a loin cloth insisted on scuttling up the Residency steps now, waving a dagger and yelling 'Infidel!' A second biscuit followed, and MacLean's patience snapped: he put down the book suddenly seized with the same perverse anger and revulsion that he had felt when he had first seen Louis feed Ria, and '*No!*' he repeated sharply to a third biscuit. But each time Ria swallowed without glancing back. On the fourth throw, MacLean's hand shot out and intercepted the biscuit, putting it into a pocket where Ria's nose followed. His tail wagged as though he understood this to be part of a game.

'Will you be still, damn you', said MacLean almost hissing

the words, and this time cuffed him lightly across the head for emphasis. In a flash Ria sunk his teeth in the hand. He released it almost immediately, cowering back as though ashamed, but his eyes were bright and wary.

MacLean stuffed the hand in his pocket quickly and glanced around, but no one was turned his way. He looked at his watch, replaced the paper bookmark, picked up his mug and knitting, and departed. Ria followed, head held high now, walking as though on the tips of his paws.

In the sick bay MacLean set out cotton wool, antiseptic, scissors, and a roll of tape in a neat row, and sat down at the desk to dress the oozing punctures on his hand. His face was very white, and his hands trembled. Suddenly he stretched it down to Ria's nose, so close that a droplet of blood smeared on a nostril 'Bad!' he said vehemently, then 'Bad!' so that he exploded the word in the dog's ear, and at the same time he cuffed the side of the woolly head again, but sharply this time.

Ria's reaction was as instantaneous as before, but this time he snarled, one lip pulled back over his teeth, before he sunk them in the hand, and this time he did not cower afterwards. For a long moment they glared at one another, almost on a level, the twice-bitten hand between them like a bone between two hackles-raised disputing dogs, one pair of eyes gleaming almost green, and the other pair glittering dark as coal. It was the man who turned away first. His face was expressionless as he attended to the wounds.

Ria remained still as a statue for a full minute, his head thrust forward and one lip still fractionally lifted, then he turned and slipped through the door to lie in his usual place outside, his head stretched on his paws and his eyes fixed unblinkingly on the man.

Through the open scuttle drifted the peaceful bah-ing sounds and all the sweet headiness of hill and moorland that had so stirred Ria a short while ago, sounds and smells that suddenly stirred MacLean now to such a sick nostalgia of remembrance that he laid his head on the sound hand lying on the desk, sick and dizzy with the too-swift transition, almost afraid to breathe, waiting for the familiar iron band to squeeze around his chest, trying to suppress all other unbidden memories before they flooded his mind and broke the dam of his reserve.

Ria whined uneasily, then came to him. He licked the blood that his own teeth had drawn from this hand that had struck him, and suddenly MacLean found that he could breathe again, all tension gone. He put his hand on the dog's head, and remembrance now was gentle and kind: *a boy riding home on the peat cart, the gorse and heather-laden summer wind gentle on his face, the sheep summer high on the hills, the lazy murmur from the burn* . . . He felt the delicate bone structure beneath his fingers, and smoothed the ears, feeling at the same time the warmth of the dog's body pressed against his legs. Perhaps he dozed for a minute.

There had been a pup, a gangling sheep dog pup, and a child had struck it again and again until it had cringed, silent and submissive before him on the ground; then the child had called it to him, clapping his hands encouragingly; then, when it was once more fawning and gambolling at his feet the child fondled and patted to see the shining adoration in its eyes, and then he had struck it again, harder this time, until it yelped; then once more the reconciliation . . .

How long had this gone on? Minutes, hours, days or years? He only knew that throughout the summer-laden wind blew steadily, even as it did today, filling him with a strange exhilaration and dreadful sorrow so that he had both laughed and cried; and then had come the fear that he could not get his breath, that the ground was falling away below him – somebody's arms had held and carried him, then the vapours of Friar's Balsam steadily steaming from a kettle somewhere drifted over all memory, the ground falling away as it was now . . . the deck below was sinking, sinking . . .

He jerked fully awake: there was a sound of boots on the

companionway at the far end of the flat. He opened the drawer and swept everything into it, and even as he did so there was a second when the world seemed to stop and there was nothing but utter still clarity, and it was as though he suddenly knew something that he had known all his life but had never wanted to know, and had resisted; in this inexorable moment he had accepted it and was resigned, knowing that there was no escape from the knowledge, and never had been.

He was sitting, tidy and composed, his jacket back on, Ria at his feet, immersed in his book, when Lessing pulled back the curtain.

Lessing was well over six feet, with enormous hands and feet, his young fresh face dominated by a pair of the most startlingly direct and guileless blue eyes. He was a most likeable youngster, so solid and dependable yet unassuming that he was already marked out for further promotion. He stood now in the entrance, seeming to fill the sick bay, and suddenly looked very awkward and unsure of himself. He was going ashore on the next liberty boat, he said; there wouldn't be anything doing in the town, but he thought he'd walk over the hills and maybe have a swim – would MacLean like to go too?

Still shocked and spent within, MacLean's defences were momentarily down; he had rejected all overtures of friendship so consistently that his solitariness was now an accepted fact and no one ever sought him out for company. He seldom went ashore, only for dockyard stores, and he had never once taken Ria. He smiled, his rare transforming smile, and said that there was nothing he would rather do more – not for the swim for he had never learned to swim, but he loved to walk, and it was a grand day for the walking; but the doctor was ashore, and he was on duty . . . and he thanked Lessing anyway for thinking of it.

Lessing seemed overwhelmed by this unusual spate of words. He stood there, awkwardly turning his cap in his hand. 'Let me take Ria then,' he said at last. He hesitated as the smile vanished but went on resolutely, 'It'll do him good to have a run – get out of this tin box for a while. Must be worse for a dog being cooped up – not even a blooming tree to think about.'

He had never once looked at the hand, but MacLean knew very well what was in his mind. For a moment, he almost reverted to his usual image and told Lessing to mind his own business, and then, almost despite himself, he heard his voice saying, 'Aye, it's an unnatural life all right. I'd be glad if you'd take him – off with you then—" to Ria who, sensing something different, pleasurable, exciting, bounded after Lessing.

MacLean looked out of the scuttle at the sunlit hills beyond the little port. He had relatives here. He had only to go ashore and telephone. His father, or his eldest brother, would take Ria for him, and in time dispatch him further north and back to Sinclair. It would be as simple as that. He could still go . . .

He picked up his cap and called after Lessing: 'Hold on a minute—'

The boy's head reappeared around the curtain, and as MacLean opened his mouth to speak Ria's face followed, his head cocked to one side enquiringly.

'I thought—' began MacLean, then, suddenly decisive, he went on; 'that this would help—' and he made a quick sketch on a notepad. 'You'll get out of the town quickly that way, then on up a sheep track until you come to a lochan—'

He watched the liberty boat speed off to the shore, then returned to his place in the sun, at peace with the world despite his throbbing hand.

Ria came back, his coat warm and fragrant still with the green growing bounty of earth that had been his for three ecstatic hours, his eyes clear and shining, his whole bearing jaunty and confident – a very different dog, as the man who greeted him could not fail to observe. Nor could the dog have failed to sense the difference in the reception from the man.

The Ark left Oban next morning, steaming down the Firth of Lorn, and when she entered the open Atlantic to turn south, MacLean came up on deck to see the last of the islands of his homeland waters and looked north. On the horizon, off the long black mass of Mull, he could just make out the lonely dot that was the holy island of Iona. He watched until it disappeared at last, and with its going some of the lightness of heart that his Margaret had brought returned to him, as though her laughter came echoing down the years. Unconsciously he smiled.

Beside him, as though bidden, Ria rose with extended forepaws in the action he had learned brought attention to himself, but which, almost as if aware of the inevitable condemnation it would receive, he had never attempted with MacLean.

He had judged his moment precisely. He looked up, his eyes round and merry, and for once MacLean looked directly down at him.

He suddenly knew that she of all people would have been the one for this dog that stood beside him now, that from her extravagance of love and gaiety she would have encouraged and abetted all antic nonsense and found a counterpart in lightheartedness. She had always wanted a dog, but she had understood, and given way to him. It had been his one denial to her.

'Behave yourself—' he said now with automatic severity, but the smile still lingered. Ria got down at once, but he wagged his tail with unabashed enthusiasm and continued to look as though he were laughing with open mouth and lolling tongue.

They turned and made their way along the deck to the stern, Ria scampering ahead unchecked. Barkis saw them from the bridge, hurled himself down, and joined them. He threw himself at Ria in his customary onslaught of pleased greeting, but Ria sidestepped him neatly at the last moment and he drew up still standing, looking very puzzled. He launched himself again, and again; he whirled suddenly one way and then the other, but always, like a toreador playing a bull, Ria evaded him in the nick of time. It built up into an exuberant game: weight and speedy cunning versus equal cunning but lightweight nimbleness.

MacLean watched, so absorbed by Ria's tactics that he was unaware of the Captain's approach until Ria fractionally misjudged his timing and nearly overbalanced to a side eddy variation of the latest whirlwind Barkis approach. 'Barkis's round, I think,' said a complacent voice behind him. But even as the Captain spoke, Ria recovered his balance, managing an amazing pirouette of an about-turn as he did so, then turned and chased Barkis who fled in mock terror before him.

'Sir!' acknowledged MacLean, straightening respectfully, but his voice was equally complacent.

Thereafter, this game was played whenever conditions of calm or inactivity allowed, with endless variations and an apparent rule between the contestants that neither should ever win. Not only did it give the dogs the exercise they so badly needed, but it was a spectator sport that fascinated Hyacinthe. She would appear like magic on some vantage point above, her green eyes huge and intense, her head following the play like an umpire at Wimbledon. Having been caught up herself once by mistake in the game she saw to it that such hideous indignity could never happen again and always chose her perch well out of dog reach.

Occasionally nowadays, bored with Louis' persistence, she had taken to seeking out Ria for diversion. Hyacinthe's favourite pastime was staring: as close as possible, she would fix her unwinking green orbs on her subject and stare and stare. No one could outstare her, and when at last the opposing eyes blinked she would stretch and purr and wind herself around her victim in triumphant pleasure.

But in Ria, who could spend hours gazing into some limitless space, she met her unswerving match. She would approach with measured tread as he lay with his head on his paws, settle herself comfortably with her front paws tucked in towards one another under her chest, then snap her eyes wide open at almost nose to nose range on Ria's. 'Like a myopic tea cosy,' as the doctor said one day, sketching the contestants. He added a pair of glasses above Hyacinthe's whiskers, her head sticking out of a furry cosy in place of a tea pot spout, and curved her luxurious ringed tail into the shape of a handle. Finally Ria was caricatured before her into nothing but a pair of huge eyes surmounted by ears, one up and one down.

'What will you do with him eventually?' he asked idly, adding another whisker to Hyacinthe.

'Return him to the man who brought him aboard, sir.' said MacLean. 'Fortunately I was able to find his name and unit from the records.'

'Most fortunate indeed,' agreed the doctor blandly. He looked up. 'It won't be easy, will it – I mean to part with him after all these months?'

There was a long pause. 'Aye,' said MacLean at last.

'What do you mean "aye"?'

There was an even longer pause. 'I mean "no",' said MacLean. 'No, sir, it will not be easy now.' The admittance was forced out of him; out at last, laid starkly bare before his own mind.

' "Brothers and Sisters, I bid you beware/Of giving your heart to a dog to tear",' said the doctor lightly, looking up in mischievous expectation of the customary acid reaction to such sentiment. 'Kipling – the "Power of the Dog",' he emphasized.

But for once he was disappointed: MacLean merely looked thoughtful as he rubbed the already gleaming top of the steriliser. 'Indeed, sir,' he said, politely.

He found the sketch on Christmas day, a freezing joyless day in mid-Atlantic, with *Tertian* plunging and rearing in mountainous seas that crashed over her decks and cascaded down every inch so that there was no dry place on board, and Christmas cheer perforce was corned beef and hard tack, for the galley fires had been extinguished.

To S. B. A. MacLean –

LATITUDE ///////// Wind NNE – Force 10

LONGITUDE //////////

MERRY, MERRY CHRISTMAS AT SEA 1940

was scrawled unevenly underneath in an obviously Force 10 hand.

He put the sketch away where other men kept photographs of families and sweethearts, in his paybook. After much thought and doubt as to whether he had lost his senses with such foolishness, he folded and packaged his latest pair of socks. The English were great on Christmas, he excused himself, as he left the package on the desk, and went off to put on all the heavy weather gear he could muster, for it was time to make the routine check of his first aid caches throughout the ship.

The life lines on deck had been rigged almost from the time they left port, stout ropes with running hand grips or tails, stretching along the length of the deck. He emerged from the doorway hardly able to stand against the force of the wind, grabbed one of the tails and started off along the pitching treacherous deck. But Ria must have slipped out at his heels, for as he turned his face away from the wind he suddenly saw him, paws resisting uselessly against the icy tilt, sliding towards the rails. At the same moment MacLean was aware of a monstrous wave towering over the port bow towards its climax. Never knowing afterwards how he had done it, he flung himself down, still hanging on to the rope tail, and managed to grab Ria's collar, his arm feeling as though it would be pulled out of its socket when the monster crashed and the foaming torrents swept along the deck. Somehow he hung on, and somehow he got Ria back inside, and there in his relief he gave way to a very natural human reaction.

'*A'choin an diabhoil!*' he roared at the shaken soaking dog, and smacked him resoundingly. And this time Ria acknowledged a rightfulness of punishment, accepting the smack with a suitably contrite rolling of his eyes, and even a placatory attempt with the end of his tail. With his soaked coat revealing every line of his slight frame, he suddenly looked very vulnerable. MacLean was totally won over. 'You devil of a dog, you,' he translated, but softly, and he carried Ria down to dry him off as much as possible with an already soaked towel from his dripping locker in a drearily sloshing mess. From the crackling wireless came the strains of 'God rest ye merry gentlemen'.

'Stupid animal followed me out,' he explained to Reid.

'It's only a bloody fool of a human who'd go up on deck unless he had to,' said Reid mildly. 'Can't your turret trip wait?'

'You don't know what that lot on the guns will get up to,' said MacLean darkly. 'Nicking my dressings for nose wipes, pinching my plaster for their corns – it's every day it's got to be or there wouldn't be a thing left.'

'Set forth, then, good Saint MacLean,' said Reid. 'I'll see that your page doesn't follow in your footsteps this time.' He bundled up the shivering dog in a jersey and stowed him – for once with no remonstration – in at his back. Usually, Ria curled up there in peaceful contentment, but this time Reid noticed that he remained strangely tense and reluctant to stay, even whining softly; there was no relaxation until MacLean returned.

But the subtle change in relationship went unnoticed by anyone else, including MacLean himself, for the transition from him imposing his will to Ria anticipating his wishes had evolved so naturally he was unaware of it. They remained to the rest of the ship's company the same undemonstrative pair together, while Ria by himself was the same amusing self-reliant diversion as always. There were few who could resist his unique blend of showmanship and humour and his remarkable ability for interpreting speech or mastering another trick had gained him a reputation for almost super-canine intelligence.

He had long drawn a self-imposed line between the upper and lower decks: the lower decks were his territory, the upper decks apparently Barkis's, and should he happen to find himself there – perhaps at the invitation of the doctor – he became very circumspect, never entering a cabin unless he were invited. Sometimes, passing by, his curiosity would get the better of him and he would stick only his head around an open door. As he was always soft-footed as a cat, this sudden appearance of a disembodied head with enormous interested eyes could be quite startling.

His interests had become legion, and had ranged beyond mere seabird, convoy or iceberg-watching to the entire ship's company, for not only was he immensely inquisitive, but he liked to keep an eye on everything aboard. MacLean's sense of the proprieties would never have recovered had he known the full extent of canine bounds transgressed. A routine that afforded great interest was the Captain's rounds, when a small unobtrusive shadow would hover at a discreet distance in the wake of the inspecting party – and thereby penetrate normally inaccessible quarters.

Once a Very August Personage indeed was piped aboard *Tertian* in port, and later met both Louis and Ria. Louis – dressed to the nines for the occasion in a sailor suit – was unimpressed by the sudden wealth of gold braid, having eyes only as always for the Captain's golden beard, but Ria's professional assessment could not be faulted: he sat up and saluted smartly on request and had his head patted by the August hand in reward. MacLean, hearing about this episode later, found it hard to look convincingly disapproving.

He had not realised how much of his heart had been given to be torn until *Tertian* returned to Devonport in early March, 1941. He was looking forward with unusual pleasure to a forty-eight hour leave, and had made plans to spend it walking on Dartmoor with Ria – the first time they would ever have gone off together. When the mail was distributed that first morning in port there was one letter for him, and the contents came as the most profound and hurtful shock.

Donald Sinclair was out of hospital and returned to his Highland glen, there to await a final medical board before being discharged from the Army. He would no longer be any good on the hills, he said, but eventually he would be running a farm instead, and now at last he could relieve Ria's benefactor of his obligation – '. . . so thoughtlessly imposed upon you. Now at last we can give the dog a settled home. Any port that you are in – if you could dispatch him from there to Glasgow, someone will pick him up there and bring him on to us . . .' He enclosed a postal order to cover any expenses involved, the ticket, and the purchase of the obligatory muzzle for 'an unaccompanied dog'.

Suddenly the world seemed very bleak, and MacLean's pleasure turned to ashes. Even fate seemed to be working against him, for within ten minutes of confiding this news to Reid, arrangements slipped easily and inexorably into place to preclude any valid deferment: Reid had returned from telephoning a sister who lived in Plymouth to say that she was travelling up to Yorkshire in a few days' time. The same train would go on up to Glasgow.

'Ria could go ashore with me this afternoon and I'll leave him with her,' he said hesitantly. 'But are you sure you have to do this? After all this time – he's part of our Ark now . . .'

'It has to be done,' said MacLean with such a wooden finality in his expression that Reid was silent.

It all happened so quickly that there was no time to brood, no time for the heaviness of his heart to be communicated, for the morning was fully occupied with routine duties. At noon he changed and went ashore with a brushed, trimmed and bright-eyed Ria who was only innocently excited at the prospect of a walk on dry land.

Once clear of the dockyard gates, MacLean handed him

over, then, feeling like a Judas, told him to go with Reid. 'Away you go for a run—' he said, forcing a reassurance. Ria was very attached to Reid and had often gone ashore with him, but now he must have sensed suddenly something disastrous. As MacLean turned away down the street he whined and struggled to follow, straining at the end of the short lead.

Reid picked him up to soothe him, but as MacLean turned the corner he heard a sound that he had never heard before – Ria barking, and barking in a high-pitched almost hysterical despair that was to haunt him for days afterwards.

He shut out the sound in the refuge of the nearest pub, the first of many that saw him that day. He drank himself into a state of solitary savage gloom such as he had not attained for a very long time – and barely made it back on board.

They were anchored out in the Sound. Soon after darkness fell, the alarms sounded and the systematic destruction of the ancient gentle town of Plymouth began. *Tertian* was a Devonport ship and many of the men had families on shore, while almost all had friends. Their own guns joining in the shore barrage, all night long they watched helplessly, sickeningly jarred by every explosion, seared by every freshly leaping fire.

Next morning those who had homes or relatives there, were given a few hours' compassionate shore leave. For some it was a thankful reunion, for others a nightmare search through the rubble-strewn streets and smouldering ruins, hopefully to neighbours' houses and the emergency centres set up for the bombed out, fearfully to hospitals or to the hastily set-up morgues.

Reid went ashore, and found his sister standing aimlessly in front of what had been her house, one of a terrace leading off the Hoe. One side was completely exposed, a gap where the adjoining house had been. All the windows were out, the roof was gone, and the kitchen extension at the back lay in an impenetrable heap of lathes and rubble. That was where

Ria had been, she informed him tearfully; fortunately she herself had been out for supper with the neighbour with whom she was now sheltering.

They could not even attempt to salvage anything from the rest of the house for there was an unexploded land-mine at the back of the row. There was nothing further Reid could do. He spent his remaining time boarding up the neighbour's shattered windows and helping where he could, then he returned to break the news to MacLean, and the only consolation he had to offer was that Ria's death must have been instantaneous.

MacLean had been standing by the rail. Without turning his head, he thanked Reid in a flat expressionless voice and continued to look across at the smouldering city under its pall of black smoke. He never spoke of Ria again.

In all too brief a time that day, those ashore were recalled urgently and all leave cancelled. Word had come through that the cruiser *Admiral Hipper* was making a sortie out of Brest, and *Tertian* was to be part of the force sent to intercept. The drawn, grey-faced searchers returned, many of them still not knowing what had befallen their families, some knowing only too well, and they slipped away in company with two other destroyers.

For days they played cat and mouse, but in the end the prey eluded them, and *Tertian* proceeded on to Gibraltar to refuel.

She passed through the gates of the Mediterranean to become a part of the Fleet there, part of the immortal annals of the Tobruk run, Mersah Matruh, Crete, and the Malta convoys – and she was never to return.

Part Three

9

The sirens sounded the red alert in Plymouth that night about 9 o'clock. For months, this had meant nothing more sinister than the approach of an enemy reconnaissance plane, or a lone afternoon raider; always, soon afterwards, the All Clear would follow. But this night, almost before the first warning notes had ebbed away, the skies were filled with the steady purposeful throbbing even as the anti-aircraft barrage and searchlights came into action, and a minute later the total bombardment of Plymouth and Devonport began. It was the first night of a terrible son et lumière display, lit by the leaping flames, the searchlights and slowly dropping flares, while the shuddering bass of the guns thundered their earthbound accompaniment to the screaming crescendos from the skies.

Ria had become used to the noises of war at sea, for even under the insulation of a mattress in a bunk sanctuary, nothing could muffle the carrying vibration of steel plates, but never had he faced the assault of violence and explosion alone, or within confining walls in the now unfamiliar surroundings of solid unmovable land.

He had been comforted by Reid's continuing familiar presence when he had been brought to this house, waiting stoically enough by the window as though expecting MacLean to appear and take him back to the Ark. Then Reid had gone, and now there was only his sister, who was kind and well-meaning, but a stranger. Then she had gone out for the evening, leaving him in the kitchen, an extension opening onto a small courtyard at the back of the house, one of a terrace leading off the Hoe. When the anti-aircraft batteries started up, there was no familiar sanctuary to which he could make his routine way; there was only himself in this small rock-still room.

When the first stick of bombs screamed down, each earth-shaking crump landing inexorably nearer, almost as though they searched him out, Ria started to his feet, and cowered against the back door; then as the last bomb began its shrieking pursuit, he bolted under the table. The bomb landed squarely between the next two adjoining houses of the terrace, slicing a path between them as cleanly as a knife through bread. The kitchen rocked and shuddered to the blast, then settled, sagging.

The deep quivering silence that followed was intruded upon, unobtrusively, almost apologetically, by a thick acrid smell, then came an awakening crash as the bricks and masonry of the next door chimney cascaded on to the roof. The timbers groaned under their burden, and with soft, shifting sighs the lathes released imprisoned plaster, pulverised now to a thick white dust that settled shroud-like on the little kitchen. Slowly, smoothly, the roof blended with the crumbling wall, widening the red gap of sky like a blind pulled back; the wall curved and trembled, then disintegrated in a shower of bricks. The floor heaved up in sympathy so that a pot slid off the stove, the rivulets of its contents almost instantly dammed by the white dust, and in slow motion the blue and white plates one by one slid off the dresser.

Now human sounds were heard, heavy running boots crunching through glass in the street beyond the courtyard, shouts, sharp orders, whistles, and a voice that said, 'Oh, Christ, oh, Christ, oh, Christ . . .' with as much humanity as a clock ticking. Beyond these noises rose the growing orchestration of the night; the multiple endless drone of aircraft, the thunder of the dockyard guns, the lighter barking of the anti-aircraft batteries on the Hoe, the high whistling crescendo then the great bass drum thumping of bombs.

Every now and then, as though some conductor had stilled every instrument with his baton, suddenly, abruptly, there fell a silence that seemed to engulf the town, then insidiously the little wounded noises would start up again, the soft sighings of flame tendrils rising to fierce hungry crackling, whispered moans that became sharp cries then shrieks, slithering slates and bricks that first plopped one by one then became a roaring avalanche of roofs and walls, the far-away bells and sirens of ambulances and fire engines drawing nearer and nearer, louder and louder.

Now the kitchen was light as day, the roof open wide to the flares swaying down from the skies, and the red glow from the burning town. The dresser topped exhaustedly across the reeling table. For a few seconds, a complete hush fell again over the small ruined world that had been the kitchen, then mounting crackles of flames rose from somewhere just beyond the jagged edges of the roof. And as though summoned from some inferno by them, the white ghostlike figure of a dog appeared from under the pile of wreckage by the table and drifted across the rubble on the floor; drifted across the door sagging on one hinge, and out into the courtyard, the eerie white of its dust-laden coat now changing from pink to red to orange from the spectroscope of orange flares against the red sky and yellow flames. The little ghost cowered trembling, until the last hinge on the door gave way and it crashed down, bringing with it a bucket that clanged across the courtyard. With that, he bolted into the street, his paws scarcely touching the ground, clearing the fence with a foot to spare.

Now he smelled fear, death, and terrible human excitement, an evil blend that sent him, eyes glazed and wild, skittering and slithering across the rubble and glass-strewn streets, shying away from the running boots of wardens and firemen, leaping over obstructions, until he reached the open spaces of the Hoe. And here he ran madly again, up the concrete paths, across the grass, from crater to crater, then down to the sea, his claws scrabbling wildly on the slimy steps as he turned away from it again. Each flare, each bomb, each salvo from the guns galvanised the desperate aimless running in the red glare of this world gone mad.

He turned from the Hoe at last and ran up the centre of the stricken burning town. A man, reeling drunk, sang in a wavering, hiccoughing tenor within the angled entrance to a draper's shop. He whistled then called but the dog turned and fled on up the street, only to reappear an instant later, running straight at the man. He swerved at the last moment and jumped into the glassless display-window of the shop, twisting through the grotesquely fallen shapes of the fashion dummies, knocking one over so that it fell with its head stuck out over the jagged glass, smiling vacuously down at the pavement. The man lurched out of his doorway, picked it up and waltzed unsteadily off down the street until a warden darted out of the shelter of a church porch and grabbed him.

In the very back of the shop, in what must have been the manager's office, crouched a cat with a mewling kitten in its mouth. It backed up against the desk as the dog ran in, and a lightning paw flashed out to rend an ear so that he turned and fled with high hysterical yipping. He ran throughout the night until, hours later, he veered crazily between the tombstones of a churchyard, and there finally collapsed under the solid sheltering wing of a marble angel toppled off a tombstone.

And while he lay there, the All Clear sounded in the dawn of a new day, and for a few minutes, silence lay like a pall across the shattered town. Nearby in a crater, the ants from a colony sliced in half scurried frenziedly, some of them carrying eggs, their dead already neatly piled some distance from the new entrances. Then all around, one by one, the dazed human inhabitants of Plymouth emerged from their burrows to survey the world that had been left to them.

The sun came up that lovely still spring morning, generous with its warmth and promise in the desolation. Its rays sought low in its rising under the marble wing and rested on the small spent creature there, so that he crawled out and licked his bleeding paws. Although his eyes still darted nervously from side to side, he was normal now with the normality of animal and newborn day; the horror of the night was over. There was no homing urge for the strange house near the Hoe; there was no one to search for, no links with anyone in the unfamiliar town; he was derelict, nameless, lost.

He stayed around the churchyard for a while, watching the weary grey people who emerged blinking from the crypt, but the terrifying wail of fire engines drove him on. He limped down a narrow street, picking his way between fragments of glass and twisted metal. The street was silent and deserted, the rows of small houses gaping at their opposite numbers, the very heart of many of them exposed.

There was no human reminder of the night, living or dead. The only body that had not been tidied away was that of an old grey-muzzled spaniel who lay as though asleep in the gutter. High up in a budding lime tree, a monstrous pair of white bloomers caught on a branch filled and danced to the light wind. Below, a robin poured out over the crater in the little front garden its proprietary song, last year's nest, blown from the deep sanctuary of the hedge, now bowling gaily along the rim. The dog sat on the sunny step before the roofless shell of a house and scratched himself, watching with mild interest a large white rabbit hopping around the next door garden. The rabbit investigated the shattered glass of a cloche, then settled down to feed, munching lettuce stolidly, its ruby eyes fixed with as little interest on the dog. A chirping cheerful family of sparrows enjoyed a dust bath nearby.

Across the street a black Labrador scrambled over a mountain of rubble, sniffing and searching. Suddenly its ears pricked, and the rudderlike tail began to swing. Possessed now by urgency, it dug with frantic forepaws, whining excitedly as the dust and rubble flew out behind.

An A.R.P. Warden appeared at the far end of the street, carrying a clipboard with the names and numbers of the inhabitants. Where possible he entered the evacuated houses, circling the gutted ones, and calling out routinely, 'Hellooo, helloooo . . . is anyone there?' The little dog watched his progress with pricked ears. The echoing 'Hellooo, hellooo . . .' rang out at last next door to where the Labrador dug, and it answered him with a continuous high barking. The man climbed over the wreckage, watched in silence for a moment, bade the dog stop – a useless command – then holding it back by the collar, he knelt down and shouted, bending his ear close to the pile.

The little dog picked his way over the rubble too, and at once his seeking nose caught the same message as the Labrador; he started digging beside the large dog, who snarled briefly at him before setting to again. The man seized a loose timber and pried aside some obstruction. He bent down again, and shouted, listened, then as feverishly as the dogs, he started digging too. 'Hold on,' he shouted, 'help's coming – just hold on . . .' And faintly now came back the assurance of life that the dogs had recognised, a whisper of sound below the imprisoning pile. Sitting back on his heels, sweat running down his blackened face, the warden pulled a whistle from his pocket and blew, until there was an answer of steel-shod boots running, and presently the wailing siren of a heavy rescue unit. This was too much for the little dog, sirens spelled disaster and confusion. Tucking his tail between his legs, he fled up the street before the banshee noise.

His ears pricking warily, conscious of much unseen, unheard, he slowed down soon to a trot, for his pads were raw with cuts. He passed a narrow house, its grubby curtains still in place on either side of the blown-in windows, the shabby door open. In and out of the door, through and out of the windows, went a quantity of cats, all of indeterminate markings, flowing backwards and forwards so continuously that they could have been four or forty. The dog was about to give the place a wide berth, for the pungent smell drifting out was offensive, when two beligerent toms erupted out of a window, snarling and spitting, locked in combat almost on top of him, and he took to his heels again. Halfway up the street, he was joined by a gambolling Alsatian puppy who leaped in clumsy playfulness at his ears.

The pup stayed with him most of the morning, occasionally plumping down to a sprawling stop, the loose skin on its fore-head wrinkled in some apparent perplexity, then trotting after again. Once they came upon a very small girl sitting on the pavement, one unbuttoned shoe on one foot, and a sock on the other, one arm through a sleeve, the other through the neck of her dress, a tearstained grubby child who had plainly attempted to dress herself. She was eating a thick piece of bread and dusty jam, and held out a hand to the puppy. It leaned against her, licking the sticky face as she hugged it, then filched the crust the moment she turned her head. She looked at her empty fingers, then she and the pup licked them carefully.

From somewhere nearby, traced by the flickering ears of the dog to the house immediately behind, a woman wept, continuously, hopelessly; and accompanying the lament, the sweet rolling arpeggios of a canary soared from the room beyond the open window. 'Mam, Mam—' called the child, but the weeping continued unbroken, and now the child's face crumpled in hungry forsaken grief. The puppy licked the salt tears from her cheek, wagging its tail cheerfully while she tried to brush it away. At last she pummelled on its head with all her strength, hammering at its round astonished eyes until it drew back abashed.

A van drove up to the entrance of the street, which was barricaded at both ends with signs LIVE BOMBS. An army officer and two men got out, and a policeman appeared. He pointed down the street, on the opposite side to where the dogs and child sat, and the soldiers set off carrying boxes of equipment. One of them saw the trio and beckoned back to the policeman who walked quickly down the street to the child and picked her up, but even as he did so his head turned to the sound of the steady weeping beyond. He called to the halted group of soldiers; then, still carrying the child, ran inside the house. Presently the woman's stifled voice answered the urgent deep tones of the man, and a few minutes later she herself emerged, carrying a fur coat and a shopping bag stuffed with clothes with one hand, her handbag and a silver trophy and teapot with the other. The policeman carried the child, a large photograph in a silver frame, a shining golden teddy bear with a red ribbon around its neck, and a wireless tucked under one arm, its cord trailing. Urging the stumbling woman on, he hurried back up the street, the puppy ambling after. The little dog sat on, his round bright eyes following them until they disappeared around the corner.

The canary sang on, forgotten; but soon afterwards the song petered out, and the street was very quiet and still, the only movement coming from the group of men half-hidden from sight in the garden on the other side of the street.

The dog picked up a few crumbs from the pavement, then trotted over to investigate. Lying exposed, deep in the soft earth which had been dug away now, was the long, finned shape of an unexploded bomb. The officer lay prone over the rim of the crater, probing delicately as he dictated through a field telephone to the two soldiers who now crouched behind a sandbagged shelter some hundred yards up the street. The dog, soundless, approached the officer from behind and examined the canine possibilities of the crater.

'. . . over,' said the officer quietly into the mouthpiece strapped to his chest. He drew his brows together as the voice through the head-phones quacked some message, 'Repeat, please,' he said, and the voice came though clearly now. 'There is a dog, repeat dog, at your right shoulder.'

He turned his head and saw the grey woolly head on a level with his own, the eyes fixed intently on some point within the crater, hind-quarters already flexed to investigate.

Very softly the man whistled under his breath, and the dog's eyes turned to meet his at six-inch radius. The dog licked the man's cheek, and in the same instant an arm came round his shoulder and clutched him in a steel grip. Taken by surprise, he reacted instinctively, twisted, and sank his teeth in the hand. But there was no relaxation in the grip, and the man backed away from the crater for some yards before rising to his feet. Carrying the squirming dog, he walked leisurely towards the soldier. The soldier's face was white.

'Shut him in the van, sergeant,' said the officer, 'and we'll start again.'

'I'd like to break its bleeding little neck,' said the sergeant. 'Another second and . . .'

The dog now lay limp and relaxed, looking from one to the other. The officer smiled down at him. The dog wagged his tail agreeably, but was handed over to the sergeant, who clamped a hand hard around his jaw, pressing his ribcage so hard that he twisted in silent pain. The officer scratched behind one ear. 'Gently with him,' he said. 'He doesn't know what it's all about.' He lit a pipe and leaned against the sandbags, an elderly untidy man, with a vague sweet face, his spectacles mended on one side with adhesive tape, his crumpled uniform terminating in a pair of plaid bedroom slippers. The soldier, viciously clamping the jaw under his hand, walked back to the van, opened the door, and threw his burden into the back; then, because he was still a very shaken man, he picked up a wrench and threw it after for good measure.

The dog crouched in the back as the door banged shut. Gradually his confidence returned and he jumped over into the driving seat. He lay across the seat with head on paws to wait, his eyes and ears alert. Nearly two hours later, he heard the sound of returning rubber-soled footsteps, and jumped into the back again, pressing himself against the side of the truck, his nose at the bottom of the crack where the door would open. He gathered himself as the handle turned,

133

and was clear of the truck a second later, running madly up the street to freedom.

He wandered on, limping and thirsty, in the hazy dust-laden sunshine. When the streets were blocked by fire engines and ambulances, he picked a passage between clumping boots that sometimes kicked him out of their urgent way, past the great heaving coils from water hydrants, through clouds of smoke, up empty streets where walls trembled above him, through choking acrid smells, and smells of death and vileness.

There was only one place he knew, and he returned to it, to the sheltering marble wing above the tombstone. And here a crazed lonely woman, wandering through the churchyard, saw him and comforted herself for a while with his reality, sitting on the grass, stroking the cold marble feathers above, and murmuring in an incomprehensible torrent to the small silent audience that paid her its grave undivided attention. A motley pack of dogs swept past in slavering courtship of a young, bewildered yet excited greyhound; trailing a leather strap from her wide collar she leaped on to a flat tombstone to snarl ritually at the most persistent of her followers, a mangy collie cur. The woman screamed at them in a flood of obscenities and the little dog fled from her to join the pack. Hours later, his ardour cooled after being set upon two or three times, he returned to his now deserted guardian angel to lick his wounds, a lip bitten through and a tattered ear.

He was there still when the nightmare started up again soon after dark, and when the first screaming hurtled down at him from the pulsing darkness he pressed back into his refuge, shuddering convulsively, until at last the noise and terror drove him to the madness of the night. This time he did not always run alone; there were other dogs that ran in terror-stricken circles too, their known world gone, instinctively packing together. Once a runaway horse came thundering up a narrow cobbled street, an old grey carthorse, galloping heavily, its flying mane and tail gallant in the unearthly

134

orange light, one opaque white eye fixed steadily ahead, the other rolling wildly. The little dog broke away from the pack as though drawn irresistibly, to run ahead, as he had once run before another old grey horse who had drawn a caravan, and who had lain kicking between the shafts until a stranger soldier had silenced the screaming with a merciful bullet. There had been a red glare, a crackling of flames, unmoving bodies that sunlit afternoon in France too; perhaps it was this that drove the little dog to his madness in the nights of bombing.

He ran with unseeing eyes before the feathered hooves striking sparks from the cobbles, until at last they thundered up a street blocked with fire engines, and there the horse wheeled, its heavy quarters skidding in the soaked debris, and it was brought down to its knees. A fireman seized the reins and encouraged it back to its feet, and it stood trembling, head flung back wildly, the nostrils dilated red to the red night sky. But what to do with an old spent horse with broken knees when there was a burning human agony and every pair of hands needed – the man lead the animal beyond the fire engines and writhing hoses until he came to a house with a garage attached. The dog trotted along behind. The garage was empty; the man tethered the horse to a workbench and ran out. The dog stretched his forepaws up to the chest of the horse, almost as though from custom; at the first touch of the light paws the horse shied clumsily, then stood, shuddering. The dog wagged his tail, and at last the horse lowered its head, whickering softly. The dog jumped on to the bench and curled up. Gradually the horse quietened, only backing clumsily and jerking its head back to the limits of the frayed tether when the bombs sounded almost directly overhead. They spent the rest of the night there.

The scrap merchant traced the runaway early next morning, and led it off down the smouldering street, followed for a while by the dog. The little procession threaded its way through the glass-strewn maze of an exhausted town that lay in a momentary respite under the calm mockery of an early morning sun that spun rainbows out of the fire hose jets and illumined the black billowing smoke with soft rosy pink. Ambulances, fire engines, rescue units and mobile canteens edged past them; men shouted angrily at them to get out of the way. They plodded on, the dog's head low as the horse's, close to its dragging hooves, until they reached the scrapyard at last, and there the man lead the horse into its stable. But when the dog would have followed, he drove him off and closed the half-door. The dog drank from a trough, then limped out into the road again where he stood indecisively for a minute or two before making his way back.

It seemed that Man was entirely preoccupied with his immediate survival and salvage and as yet his compassion could encompass only the humans of his shattered world. Often the mere animal offence of being concerned only with their own business of survival brought about the equally primitive reaction of the hand reaching for the nearest missile, or the toe of a boot finding its mark. That a hungry scavenging dog would feed on the overturned contents of a meat safe while ten yards away lay the body of the one who planned to cook those contents offended by its very reasonableness; that rats should emerge sleek and prosperous from the same cellars where man now sought refuge, or a spider painstakingly spin a web across his newly blown-in windows – all such behaviour had somehow become a terrible violation. The uncaring abstraction of tied dogs, the fluttering of mounting sparrows – these too were such unendurable desecrations that even the exultant nocturnal scream of a copulating cat could seem more noisome than a descending bomb.

The little dog, after some bitter experiences, was well aware of all this; although he must have hungered for human company in his lonely terror he learned to keep his distance from it. He stayed roughly around the same area during those days, foraging in dustbins or the wreckage of shops and houses. He was mainly attracted by the heavy rescue crews working round the clock to free survivors trapped under the debris of collapsed houses, for the reward of what had lain beneath the wreckage that first morning when he had dug with the black Labrador had apparently given much pleasure to man. Perhaps in the expectation of further approbation he would often try to join in other digging operations; but always he was driven away by angry voices, sometimes more forcibly and painfully by thrown bricks from those who interpreted his diligence as a morbid desecration; sometimes he tried to remove mountains of rubble by himself, knowing certainly that beneath it lay the living reward that man sought elsewhere, but pointing out its presence in vain.

In the late of afternoon of the third day, cowed and slinking now with furtive wary eyes, he wandered further afield to a residential area on the outskirts of the town, and there, rifling through the already well-rifled contents of a dustbin blown into the orchard adjoining a large garden, he paused, one paw lifted, sniffing the air, his ears upright. He limped through the garden, following some scent or sound, until he came to a building at the bottom of the garden, a coach-house converted into a garage. The windows were blown in and most of the roof down, but the walls still stood sturdily. To the right of the closed double doors was the original stable door, half open, and the little dog, after hesitating for a moment, edged in warily.

The interior was a tangled mass of beams, lathes and slates, and he approached it with much caution, low to the ground, his nose still working busily. Where a small inverted V of access to the pile had been formed by two beams he paused, his tail moving fast, ears cocked and head to one side, whining excitedly. Now he inserted his head into the V, his slight body followed, and like a wraith he infiltrated the narrow tunnel. It widened out after a few yards to a small clearing, the roof formed by a jumble of precariously balanced timbers. An arm protruded from below, lying along a length of board, and as the dog crawled towards it the fingers opened and closed as though beckoning.

Delighted with his find, he licked the hand, then wagged his tail when a weak muffled voice from below responded to his action. Questing around for access he tried to tunnel down through a mass of plaster board to which remnants of paper and yellowed magazine pictures of horses still adhered. As he dug, the vibration loosened part of the delicate spillikin construction of the pile, and from somewhere above there was a groaning shift of weight followed by a heavy resettlement of timbers, then a small avalanche of plaster. The immediate V remained above, but the little entrance tunnel was now gone. The dog yelped as a heavy board pinned one paw; he pulled desperately, the yelping changing to a higher pitch with the pain. The paw tore free at last; whimpering, he fell to licking his mangled toes.

The weak disembodied voice below whispered for a while, then grew silent, but the hand still moved wearily as though in search, until at last the fingers found and closed upon the other paw, tracing the pads and nails, circling the delicate hocks. He licked the fingers perfunctorily and returned his attention to the injured paw. A glimmer of light high up in the tangled pile slowly faded as darkness fell. The bleeding staunched at last, exhausted with pain and hunger, he laid his head on the other paw, his muzzle resting lightly on the hand. The fingers moved out and up past the matted hair on the crown of his head, then to the sensitive hollow behind his ears. Sometimes the arm was withdrawn for a while, but the voice continued, sometimes speaking, sometimes singing; sometimes it called out high and continuously, when he would whine or lick the hand as though in response to a call.

Gradually he and the hand grew weaker, both lying listlessly for hours at a stretch. By the evening of the second day the hand had gone and the voice was long silent. He could no longer lift his head, and his eyes were blind and sealed with a yellow discharge. He lay without movement, as though awaiting the end with patient resignation, only the occasional flick of one ear to sudden creaks above betraying the will to live.

On the late morning of the third day he raised his head and momentarily freed the other – then suddenly he pushed back on one foreleg to his haunches and broke into a high wild barking.

10

Alice Tremorne had been trapped for two nights and days when the dog found her. She had been alone in the house as Miss Carpenter, her companion help, was away on a week's holiday, and the daily help had left soon after putting the evening meal in the oven. After listening to the nine o'clock news, restless and so bored with her own company that she had even cleared away the supper dishes for the first time in her life, Mrs Tremorne suddenly thought of sloe gin. At the beginning of the war she had put up several bottles. They should be pleasantly aged by now, maturing in the inspection pit of the garage, a place which she had found, after much trial and error, maintained an excellent temperature for her home-made wines. She would tell Janet Carpenter to fetch a sample bottle when she returned . . .

But the more she thought about the sloe gin, the more she wanted to try it now; how very inconsiderate of the woman not to have foreseen this wish. Why should she have to wait five days before it was realised? She could not. She would not. *She would fetch some herself* – she would show Carpenter she was not indispensable. It would be interesting to see how the Elderflower '37 was faring too. Wincing, but still majestic, Mrs Tremorne rose stiffly to her feet.

Taking a small torch, a fur wrap, and her stick from the hall cupboard, she shuffled slowly down the path to the garage, grimly enjoying the outing, savouring each detail of the hazards of steps and path to relate to Carpenter in due course.

She hoped she would be able to manipulate the bottles, for her hands as well as her legs were stiff and swollen with arthritis. Anticipating difficulty, she had put two small bottles and a funnel in the string bag over her arm so that at least she could transfer some of the contents in the garage itself.

Where the cobbles had been taken up from the stable yard, the surface had been paved; very easy to negotiate, even for an elderly woman who normally never set foot outside without her companion's arm being available. But when she opened the garage door and shone the light around, she realised that she had forgotten the fitted boards covering the pit. She would have to remove the ones over the steps. Her knees twinged at the thought. But Mrs Tremorne was not one to turn back from her determined course; somehow she managed to lever up enough boards. Puffing and panting, giddy with the effort, cursing Carpenter, she now realised that it would be sheer foolhardiness to attempt the cement steps of the pit without a handrail. She decided to investigate instead the deep cupboard in which the matured bottles of Elderberry, Ginger and Blackcurrant wines were kept, under the stairs leading to the loft.

Outside the sirens wailed, such a normal event almost every evening since the war had begun that she took no notice. She unlocked the door, closing it carefully behind her before switching on the light. The neat rows of labelled bottles filled her orderly soul with pleasure, dating back to – let me see when – she adjusted her pince-nez and bent closer. It was at this precise moment that she realised the sirens had heralded business this time; the anti-aircraft defences ringing the town burst out into an excited crackling, and now the great thudding of the naval guns from the dockyard joined in. Above all this was another seldom heard but unmistakable noise, a very unpleasant noise indeed, with the spaced finality of its dreadful thuds rattling her bottles and sending the suspended light-bulb into a crazy flickering dance: *those unspeakable Germans were actually having the effrontery to bomb Plymouth.*

Mrs Tremorne switched off the light, and re-opened the cupboard door. The open garage door now framed a bright orange sky across which searchlight fingers moved, and a garden illuminated as clearly as a stage setting. A flare floated down towards the paddock beyond, and as she watched her fascination changed to irritation as the bright unearthly glow revealed unseemly mounds of fresh mole-hills on her lawn. There was a sudden clanging as fragments of metal rained down on the path, an unpleasant pattering on the roof above. She found herself longing for the comfortable haven of her armchair in the shelter of the cellar stairs of the house, three comforting floors and the concrete stairs overhead.

Then her world was filled with a rushing screaming noise like an express train coming straight at her. Arthritis and all, Mrs Tremorne dropped to the floor and lay flat, her head buried in her arms. The stone floor rocked, she felt as though all air were being sucked out of her body, her head exploding, then her body became strangely weightless. Without in any way feeling conscious of her passage across the garage, she had been neatly picked up and as neatly deposited on the straw on top of her own bottles at the bottom of the pit. At the same time, almost as though she had activated some lever, the roof collapsed, the first beams to fall straddling the pit, and so supporting the remainder that fell in crazy order on top. Terribly shaken, her head spinning, her eardrums thudding, Mrs Tremorne lay on her straw mattress and wondered if this was the end. Before she could find out, she dropped off into unconsciousness.

When she came to some hours later, lying there with her arms by her sides, in thick black silence, she thought that she was in her coffin, additional proof being that when she spoke up indignantly to say that there had been some mistake, she heard no words. She resigned herself, with black fury, to eternal rest.

After a while, she became conscious of sharp things boring through the straw, like fakirs' nails into her back, and memory returned: the tops of her wine bottles. She lifted her arms then each leg cautiously in turn; everything worked. She felt herself carefully, but could not find even a scratch; her shoes had been blown off, but she still clutched the torch in one hand, the string bag was still over her arm, the medicine bottles were intact inside. After much painful effort, she managed to get to her feet, resting her elbows on a cleared space at floor level. She saw now that there were occasional chinks of red light in the otherwise impenetrable mass over her. She swept the beam of the light around the roof of her prison and saw that even if she had had the strength to remove some of the obstruction, the balance was so delicately conserved that she might well loosen a key support and bring the whole jumble crashing down. She would have to resign herself to waiting. Conserving her light, her strength. Thank goodness, even although the night was not cold, she had put on her cape. It irritated her very much that she had no one except herself to blame for her predicament, this unnerving silence – only those dreadful Germans, and she concentrated all her hate on them.

She did not know when the All Clear sounded at last in the early morning; she did not even know if it was day or night, only that she was now very cold and ached in every bone. She shouted and shouted not knowing that her voice had become a whisper, and tears of fury and weakness furrowed down her dusty cheeks. Falling silent at last from sheer exhaustion, she realised that the A.R.P. post at the corner of the street where the listed occupants of all the houses around were kept, would probably check the house only. Knowing that Miss Carpenter was away – one of the wardens was her cousin – and finding no evidence of Mrs Tremorne (if only she had not been so altruistic with that supper tray . . .) they would assume that she had gone out for the evening. They would never think of looking in the garage, for everyone knew that she was unable to get around without assistance. But the daily would come at 9 o'clock, Mrs

Tremorne reassured herself, she would know, she would come searching. . . .

But no one came. She had no idea of the passage of time for her watch had stopped. She moved some bottles to form a straw nest. Sometimes she fell into an exhausted sleep, sometimes she forced herself to move her arms and legs and stand leaning on the edge of the pit, shouting. Sometimes, lightheaded, she sang, her fingers pressed over her vocal chords to assure herself that sound was indeed coming forth. Thirsty, she remembered the sloe gin; transferring some to a small bottle in total darkness occupied her for a long time. She spilled a lot before she learned the art, but the result – taken strictly medicinally – was very comforting. And the more sips she took, the more it seemed that her hearing was returning; she could even hear occasional sounds of traffic from the road beyond the garden. But they only increased her feeling of a terrible loneliness and desertion – the rest of the world going about its business, uncaring of Alice Tremorne.

It was in one of these more lonely moments, during her second night if she had known it, that as she leaned against the pit edge, and clenched and unclenched her fingers against their growing stiffness, she suddenly heard an unfamiliar creaking in the immediate timbers. She shone the weak beam of the light in this direction, calling for help in a husky whisper, then suddenly, out of nowhere came the warm wet touch of a tongue on her finger. Instinctively repelled she jerked her arm back; then as though to reassure her, she heard a soft whining, and knew that this was not the repulsive questing of a hopeful rat. Her fingers moved again to touch a muzzle, ears, to be covered again by an eager tongue – it was a dog that had come out of the blackness to her, the only living thing that knew or cared, apparently, that she still existed.

Unfamiliar tears of gratitude welled up in Mrs Tremorne's eyes. When the pile shifted, and high agonised yelps followed she forgot her own splitting head and aching bones; she longed only to comfort this warm miraculous link with life, to show it by the soft stroking of her fingers how much she cared. From that moment, Mrs Tremorne determined that if she had to spend another month here, living on gin in total darkness, she would somehow come out of it and see the reality of this small creature that had risked its life to come to her need out of the terrible night.

It was undoubtedly the same sloe gin that put her there in the first place that brought her out alive again, for it was to be another two days before she was found by the conscientious Janet Carpenter who had cut short her holiday to come back when she could receive no satisfaction on the telephone, the lines being down. She had arrived only that morning, after travelling for two nightmarishly slow days. She had been unable to find the daily help who had promised so faithfully to look after Mrs Tremorne. She had vanished without a trace, padlocking her cottage behind her, and for a while Miss Carpenter thought Mrs Tremorne might have vanished with her, to some safer hideout in the country. She knew that her mistress would not have gone out with friends that evening, as the warden suggested, for the simple reason that she had no friends. No one even liked her sufficiently to ask her out and put up with her overbearing bitterness for an evening. But it never occurred to her to think beyond the house at first; Mrs Tremorne elsewhere, solo, was unthinkable.

It was not until after her fruitless investigations that she came out into the garden to survey the wreckage and heard a faint muffled barking. Puzzled, she traced it to the garage. Plainly there was a dog trapped somewhere in that pile; but how to set about getting it out was another matter, for the whole structure above it looked perilous in the extreme. She sniffed the air; it smelled as though some Bacchanalian orgy had recently taken place. The cupboard under the stairs hung drunkenly, one hinge on the shelves buckled and a pile of broken bottles covered in white dust lying below. On top was a curiously familiar shape under its coating of dust. Picking her way carefully over she picked it up: she held Alice Tremorne's ivory-headed cane, as much a part of her normally as though it were an extension of her left arm. Janet Carpenter turned and ran for the A.R.P. post.

They uncovered, piece by precarious piece, first the dog, a small white shadow of a dog who gazed blindly up at them from thickly encrusted eyes behind a matted fringe of hair, dusty white save for the contrasting red of a clean licked, mangled fore-paw, so light that as it was lifted out it seemed there could be nothing but dry bones within the enveloping whiteness. The man who held it was conscious of the sweet sickly smell of infection, the dry hot skin below the coat. Nevertheless, it acknowledged man's presence by a brief quivering of the end of its tail. He laid it on the floor and they set to again for the urgent, yet frustratingly slow uncovering of Mrs Tremorne's body.

It was unveiled at last. Stretched out neatly on a bed of straw, her head pillowed on a flat square of empty bottles, hands folded tidily on her chest under the sable cape, her stockinged feet together, Mrs Tremorne lay. The string of pearls on the massive shelf of her bosom moved up and down with peaceful regularity. Even as they gazed upon her, the slack lower jaw dropped another fraction, she hiccoughed gently, and then a loud imperious snore fell upon their astonished ears.

She was taken to hospital, where – almost incredibly for a seventy-six-year-old semi-invalid – no damage other than a bruising which discoloured almost her entire body had been found, and now it was a matter of time and rest only.

The overworked nursing staff hoped fervently that the time with them would be brief, for she was a despotic bell-ringer of a patient. The first thing she had asked for when she recovered from her monumental but merciful hangover was the dog, her rescuer, in whom, as she declared, had lain her salvation. Miss Carpenter, hovering dutifully by the bed, was bidden to find to find out about this canine hero forthwith. What did it look like? It was just a dog, a small dog, Miss Carpenter said, remembering with aversion the limp, dirty, blood-stained bundle, but adding only that it appeared to have a shortish tail and longish ears. Mrs Tremorne regarded her with scorn.

'It was a miracle,' she said, her words still somewhat slurred, 'I held ish paw and strength flowed out, poshitively *flowed* out . . .' Her glazed eyes glared from the pillow, challenging anyone to dispute the source of the miracle working flow, and Miss Carpenter left to track it down.

She was able to report next day that one of the rescue team had taken the dog home with him, and his wife was looking after it; its eyes were open, the wound on the paw was clean, but possibly there were internal injuries or severe shock for the animal seemed to have lost the will to live – it simply lay in a box without stirring, and was kept going only by the efforts of the woman with spoonfuls of warm milk laced with precious whisky.

She must be suitably rewarded, and a vet must be called immediately, commanded Mrs Tremorne – two, three vets if necessary. A taxi must be summoned so that dog could be installed at The Cedars straightaway. Carpenter must go forth and – here was her alligator bag – set the machinery in motion; a dog basket, the best, to be bought; leads, brushes, bones and tempting dog delicacies – dogs liked liver, she knew: fetch then, quantities of liver . . .

Liver was very hard to get nowadays, offered Miss Carpenter apologetically. 'Tell Hobbs the Butcher I wish liver,' said Mrs Tremorne, weakly but majestically. The butcher's had received a direct hit, Carpenter had heard. 'What has that to do with Hobbs obtaining liver?' enquired Mrs Tremorne in genuine surprise.

It was useless explaining; no one tried. The war to Alice Tremorne was simply an interlude of personal inconvenience.

Miss Carpenter departed dispiritedly into the ruins of the shopping centre.

'Good dog, good little doggie,' mumbled Alice Tremorne, drifting off again. 'Did it hurt then? Poor little doggie . . . never mind . . . Alice is here . . .'

II

If miraculous strength had flowed out of the dog's paw to Alice Tremorne, now the procedure was reversed and strength flowed back through every means that the hand dipping into its alligator bag could provide. The little dog entered a new stage of his life that held everything a solicitous parent might give its child, a life of extreme contrast to all he had ever known, in its quiet stability and ordained pattern of day following upon day. By the time Mrs Tremorne was allowed home to her well-aired bed, still stiff and sore, he was installed in a basket (the best) in her bedroom, his coat brushed to gleaming point, his hair tied back from his eyes with a red ribbon, and combed to a silken length that would have sent MacLean rushing in shame for scissors. The hair around his delicate hocks had been shaved to match the area around the injured paw over which a baby's blue bootee was drawn to hold the dressing in place. He hopped on three legs, and several times a day Miss Carpenter, mouth buttoned into a thin line, clipped a leash on to the lightest and finest of red collars and took her charge for an airing in the garden. After the first day of Mrs Tremorne's homecoming she no longer returned him to the basket, but lifted him – her lips by now almost invisible – into the fastness of Mrs Tremorne's bed, who then drew her pink silk eiderdown tenderly over.

At first he had hardly stirred, lying with dull apathetic eyes that were wide open yet seemed to focus on nothing. When they closed and he slept briefly, his body twitched convulsively, and then Mrs Tremorne would reach out to pat and talk the reassuring baby talk that she had never used in her life but which seemed to come naturally to her now, until he lay quiet again. As the days passed, his tail gradually stirred more and more, his eyes cleared and focused, his ears rose fractionally – until one day she woke from a light sleep to find him lightly brushing her arm with one paw, his eyes beaming with interest. Yet another indomitable little dog had risen from the ashes.

Now to find a name for him. It seemed to Alice Tremorne that if she tried enough words she might run into a chance combination of vowels that would sound near enough to the dog's ears. Propped up against her pillows, her anonymous audience's eyes fixed upon her with unwavering attention, she started off by running through all the fictional or traditional canine names that she could remember: Rover, Fido, Blackie, Spot, Kim . . . She sent Carpenter down to the library: Garm, Argus, Owd Bob, Beautiful Joe, Luath, Beowulf, Greyfriars Bobby . . . She ran through name after name but none met with any recognition. Matthew, Mark, Luke, John . . . she persevered: Tinker, Tailor, Soldier, Sailor . . . She was about to dip into the telephone book when she remembered John Peel and his hounds.

'Yes, I ken John Peel, and Ruby too!/ And Ranter and Rover/ . . .' She trailed off; no, it wasn't Rover, it was . . . Raver? Ringworm? She started off at the beginning again, hoping to get carried along unconsciously: 'Do ye ken John Peel,/Wi' his coat so gay,' she sang determinedly, only to get stuck again at Ranter. It was very irritating to one who prided herself on her memory.

She was still at it when Miss Carpenter arrived to take the dog out, and when commanded to make a duet she outran Mrs Tremorne convincingly: 'Ranter and Ringwood,/Bellman and True!' she continued in a surprisingly sweet soprano.

It was irritating to be bested; but as Mrs Tremorne repeated the new names, suddenly the ears before her rose and flickered and the round eyes lit up in seeming recognition. She repeated the names, and this time the dog jumped off the bed and sat quivering expectantly, his eyes never leaving her face. It was Bellman that excited him, but she soon found that the first half of the word had the same effect: 'Bell!' she said, '*Bell* – good Bell!' and each time she spoke, the dog's tail wagged more furiously.

'You see,' she said triumphantly, 'that's his name – Bell! Time for walkies then, my darling Bell—' She gazed down dotingly

In glum silence, Carpenter clipped on the lead. Then, almost unheard of, she produced an opinion of her own. 'I think Bell's a silly name for a dog,' she said. 'It sounds like a girl one way or a chime the other.' She sniffed.

Mrs Tremorne was not used to mutiny, but she quelled it now with cunning ease: 'Neither the feminine nor the ding dong,' she said with lofty dismissal, 'but *Bel*, who – as I am sure you will remember – was the god of heaven and earth in Babylonian mythology.'

Many years addiction to *The Times* crossword had paid off. Bel he became, despite Carpenter sniffs, the sound of the name near enough to the one to which he must have responded for so many years before he became Ria.

Measure for measure, he returned the love and care lavished on him, and all his uninhibited affection and natural gaiety, so long denied, returned. He filled out to an attractive alert healthiness, becoming in the process the closest thing to a poodle to which the united efforts of his mistress and a kennel maid skilled in the art could clip and comb him, the dark curls of the outer coat stripping down to a pale, almost lavender, grey. The mutilation of his toes left him with a permanent slight limp but did not seem to inconvenience him at all.

The gardener, the milkman, the postman, every tradesman who came to the door – in fact, any human who entered the house or garden – was greeted with enthusiastic interest, and if it were not immediately returned he would stand on his hindlegs to draw attention to the oversight.

Soon, even the reluctant Miss Carpenter, who had lived only for retirement one day with an undemanding canary, fell under his spell. She no longer looked so haunted, for now that Mrs Tremorne had an all-engrossing interest, the spotlight of attention had shifted, and an atmosphere of almost cosy warmth gradually permeated the normally gloomy house with their mutual absorption. Suddenly one day she became Janet. Bel loved her, and more and more she enjoyed his company and the interest he brought to her formerly solitary walks. But undoubtedly the one who received his full devotion was the one whom he had found himself, his own human bounty, Mrs Tremorne.

He seemed to be completely content in his role of the perfect companion to her; a dog who had quickly learned to interpret yet another vocabulary, who roused no antagonism in other dogs, whose presence did not raise the hair or flatten the ears of cats, friendly with all worlds; a perfect dog, obedient, fastidiously clean, with faultless manners, even towards food, for at first he would eat nothing, however tempting, unless she were eating too. To all appearances a dog for old ladies to pamper, who could fit right into a gentle purposeless life as though he had known no other; a chameleon little dog. Yet there were times when Mrs Tremorne felt that it was like living with some kind of ghostly X, the unknown quantity – who and whatever had formed his life before he came to her. There was a certain excitement in finding new clues towards the solving, but mostly they only tantalised further with fragmentary glimpses of an unshared world.

There were times when he lay for hours on top of the garden wall, watching the world that passed below as though he were waiting to recognise some familiar form. Watching him herself, Mrs Tremorne gradually discovered the pattern of his interests: the clip-clop of a horse-drawn milk van or coal cart always brought the most eager attention; servicemen, and sailors in particular, always aroused attention; children were accorded only a flicker of interest, passing dogs no more than a polite ritual acknowledgement. But this knowledge only added up to the questionable composite of an equestrian batchelor sailor for a former owner, and was not much help. He made many friends among the regular passers-by. They would stop and have a word with him, and he would receive their attentions with dignified polite interest, but he would never jump down off the security of his garden wall. He also made an excellent early warning system, for minutes before the sirens wailed to the approaching throb of German raiders he had abandoned the wall to make for the furthermost corner of the shelter under the kitchen stairs. A bonfire one day in the garden terrified him into this refuge as well.

There were the occasional times too when he lay listless and unresponsive, his eyes infinitely sad and faraway. One afternoon, eerily, he had sat up suddenly, thrown his head back and howled, a high haunting sound that had rung in Mrs Tremorne's ears for days afterwards, unable to gauge at the depths from which such sorrow must find outlet. Sometimes she found herself almost willing him to speak, to tell her what he was so obviously imploring her to do on those occasions when he would sit before her, or crouch at the top of the stairs, tense, searching her eyes, straining every nerve to get his message across as to the part she must play in some ritual . . . 'Darling Bel, what *is* it?' she would implore. 'What are you trying to tell me?'

'Sit up!' and 'salute' and 'catch' had been translated into immediate action, and she had discovered that he would toss and catch biscuits balanced on his nose, but whatever other time-honoured canine trick command she gave – speak, say please, roll over, jump – a puzzled shadow only would flit over his eyes, and it seemed as though she would never find the key words that would unlock any further response.

But as the bond between them grew, his quivering need to communicate became stronger.

One day, he rose to his hindlegs in a bid to keep her attention longer. She took his forepaws. The wireless was playing Irish jigs, and she laughed down at him, moving his paws in time to the music. 'Come on, my darling,' she said, 'dance with me—' She moved three stiff close steps to the right, and then to the left, and he followed her. 'One, two, three,' sang Mrs Tremorne to her eager little partner, 'and a one, two, *three*—' Breathless, she let his paws go, but to her astonishment he circled on, nodding his head and pawing the air in a quaint little dance.

Her reaction, of course, was one of unmitigated admiration and enchantment as she clapped her hands – and relief too, for it was as though some barrier had been broken down. Her pleasure was so patent that thereafter he volunteered this performance from time to time; but only, she noticed, when the need to communicate or demonstrate affection to her became so overwhelming that he had no other recourse, a unique bestowal of himself. A barrier had indeed been broken down but she could never know how strong and deeply entrenched it had been.

Because she wanted more than anything else to participate in the life that now ran with hers, she forced herself to walk more and more so that she could go further afield to the garden and watch her darling's enjoyment there. Unheeding of the almost impossible goal she had set for her arthritic legs, her ambition was to take Bel for a proper country walk one day. Sometimes she ached in every other part of her body as well, but whitefaced with effort, she persevered, and was rewarded in more ways than one, for not only did she begin to feel better physically, but through Bel she made daily contact with the outside world. She had actually been seen at the far end of the orchard talking over the fence – about Bel naturally – to her neighbour. But she was so slow that she decided he must have more from her than this sedate accompaniment; he must have more outdoor pursuits and more interests to keep his mind off himself and overcome these lonely listless periods.

She planned to buy a ball for a start; he would chase it, retrieve it, she would throw it up in the air and over gates and he would jump and leap and have all the exercise she could not give him.

Fortunately she was spared the bending and stretching of these activities. That afternoon, she and Bel had reached the far end of the garden at their customary tortoise pace when suddenly he stopped, his ears pricked, tense and quivering. Then he gathered himself and shot like an arrow down through the hedge, across the small orchard beyond, and leaped at the barred gate to the paddock. He paused there, poised on the top bar, his tail moving in the strange nervous vibration that was his version of the more usual wagging of other dogs. Clinging on with his front paws, his tail moving more rapidly than ever, he looked so like a fluffy hovering dragonfly that Mrs Tremorne laughed out loud.

Now she saw the object of his excitement, her neighbour's donkey, the long-retired Fred who grazed her paddock from time to time – he must have been turned out there again only today. She watched Bel streak across the grass, then slow down to a halt a few feet away, his excitement apparently diminished. However, he sniffed around, examining from every angle, returning with his nose the compliments of the donkey as it gently nudged his head. He crouched, sprang, and dropped lightly on the shaggy back. Fortunately it was not the first time that Fred had felt an unexpected weight there; fifteen years of children had accustomed him to almost anything. Mrs Tremorne leaned on her cane and revelled in the light-hearted spectacle of Bel, his mouth open, pink tongue lolling as though in laughter, his forepaws so rigid before him that they looked as though they pushed back his head and trunk. Fred moved off slowly, cropping the grass, the small motionless rider still on his back.

When Mrs Tremorne called at last Bel came running immediately, his eyes still alight with excitement. She filed away another clue towards the unknown X. After this there was no problem about outdoor interest: if not bound for a session on the wall he would trot off briskly in search of Fred, sometimes pottering around the paddock in his company, sometimes lying close by as the donkey whiled away the long summer afternoons in the shade of the trees, sometimes bounding in a beautifully co-ordinated arc on to the broad patient back, there to dream with head thrown back, erect and totally still. Yet if Mrs Tremorne tried to persuade him to repeat this leap to order, he would simply sit before her, looking more and more puzzled the more she exhorted.

The withdrawn hours became fewer and fewer as the timeless weeks stretched into months within the garden walls, the war intruding only in domestic inconvenience, sporadic sorties to the air raid shelter, or through the impersonal voices of the BBC bringing news of the disastrous world that lay beyond:

'Today's official reports from Singapore indicate a grave situation ... our troops have again had to fall back ...'

'Dreadful, dreadful,' said Mrs Tremorne.

'A great sea and air battle is going on in the English Channel ... Scharnhorst, Geneisenau ... Prinz Eugen ...

The cost to us: six Swordfish aircraft are missing ... twenty bombers ... sixteen fighters ...'

'That *unspeakable* little Hitler—' said Mrs Tremorne.

The convoys battled on against the ever multiplying U-boat packs, such a terrible toll exacted that rationing became even more stringent. A strange tinned fish called snoek – popularly supposed to have originated in very old Rhodesian rain barrels – made its appearance on ration points. Whalemeat was expensive but required no points. Succulent slabs of horsemeat destined for British dogs were dyed blue to discourage human consumption. However, 'The introduction of soap rationing will reduce the consumption of soap by one-fifth,' declared the 9 o'clock news voice. Lord Woolton created his Wartime Pie.

Terrible, *terrible!*, said Mrs Tremorne when he revealed its ingredients.

But it was only when she was faced with the prospect of one egg per fortnight and an ounce of butter to spread over seven slices of morning toast that the full impact of the war was brought home. She was unable to dismiss the inconvenience any longer; it was clearly here to stay, and for some time. Unable to do anything about the butter, she turned her attention to a long range solving of the egg problem: they would keep hens. Fortunately Janet showed unexpected enthusiasm for this project. Even more happily, yet another interest was provided for Bel. Six day-old chicks were bought; for the first few days they were reared in the kitchen under a lamp in a box, and under the unwavering gaze of Bel who appeared to be almost mesmerised by them. When they huddled together under the lamp for a brief sleep he relaxed; when they awoke, their cheepings brought him scurrying back. When they were let out they followed him around as though he were a mother hen; and if he lay down they climbed all over him. His retinue persisted even when they were grown birds and had the run of the orchard and, for a while, the garden. They would converge on him from all quarters with hysterical clucking excitement when he appeared, and were greatly frustrated when their wings were clipped and they were no longer able to fly up and perch beside him on the donkey's back. Mrs Tremorne was greatly amused by his feathery following until they took to searching him out in the house, perching on windowsills, peering through, gaining access through any open door or window. After she and Bel had woken up one morning to the sound of their triumphant voices outside the bedroom door, they were exiled from the garden.

Now Bel's days were full indeed, and by the time a year had passed and the months of the second were marching on, he was indirectly contributing to the war effort as well, for in a combination of patriotism – stirred into activity by the fall of Singapore where she had once lived – and the effort to arrest the stiffness of her fingers in order to groom him, Mrs Tremorne had learned to knit. Slowly and painfully she knitted for the Naval Comforts Fund, working her way up through the endless tedium of scarves to balaclavas and mitts, and then the ultimate triumph of socks. When the articles were collected the names and addresses of the knitters were pinned on, and sometimes they were despatched this way. Months later Mrs Tremorne received acknowledgment of her labours from two of the recipients, a Wren stationed in Scapa Flow, into whose hands a pair of mitts had found their way, and a Leading Seaman who might well have been on the Arctic convoy routes from his description of the cold.

Mrs Tremorne was strangely touched by their letters; for the first time she was in personal contact with the war. So touched, that from now on she and Janet saved from their rations of sugar, margarine and dried fruits, and one day two cakes were despatched.

She wrote regularly to her protégés, long inconsequential letters totally unrelated to the war; about what was coming up in the garden, the hens, a book she had read – but always the longest paragraphs were about Bel, and Bel's day to day activities. Perhaps her age and infirmity were apparent in her writing, perhaps the youngsters to whom she wrote appreciated this other-worldliness in the midst of service life, or perhaps she was just exceptionally fortunate, but she received many long letters in return, and even from time to time small presents. The one which she particularly treasured was a diagonally-sliced sliver of tusk, minutely engraved with an endless procession of infinitesimal dogs. She had it set into a brooch and never wore any other.

If her life had been completely altered by Bel's coming, so was Janet Carpenter's, who looked ten years younger – almost within five years of her actual thirty-four. Having looked after her elderly ailing parents until they died, she had been untrained for any job. Unable, because of a slight congenital heart defect, to escape into the more colourful life of the women's services, she had resigned herself to the grey future of a light-duties companion. Now that Mrs Tremorne was so occupied, and content to be left in the company of Bel, she had nerved herself to ask if she might join one of the voluntary services, and now slaved most happily two afternoons and two evenings a week in a railway canteen.

She proved to be an unexpectedly amusing raconteuse, and brought back a breath of outside life each time as she regaled Mrs Tremorne with her various encounters over the coffee urns. Mrs Tremorne, eager to expand her Bel audience, encouraged her to invite lonely or stranded young service men and women back to The Cedars.

At Christmas, by now well-launched into under-counter or behind-haystack deals, she procured a magnificent turkey, wine, and even crackers, and eight young people sat down to an unforgettable dinner. Afterwards, one of them produced a pennywhistle, another a concertina, and they sang carols. Then, as though to put the final seal of pleasure on this happiest of days, Bel judged his moment, and rose to perform his solemn little dance to the music.

It had been some time since he had expressed himself this way to Mrs Tremorne, and as she watched him circle now with nodding head and outstretched paws, she saw that his eyes sought hers with the same strange intensity of those first weeks. At that moment, with a sudden jealous stab of help-lessness, as though she had somehow failed him, she knew without doubt that this was only a part of a presentation: it should go on, but it could not for something was missing, and she could not provide it. Everything else in his life she could provide, but not this release that belonged to someone else.

She did not speak of this to Janet; if she had become such

an absurd old woman that she was jealous of a ghost then it was better to keep it to herself. She comforted herself in bed that night by thinking of all his ways that belonged only to her, that had no part of any other life but The Cedars; how he brought her stick, carried up the morning newspaper, retrieved a fallen ball of wool, searched out the sites of cunningly concealed eggs – and a dozen examples that had sprung from her alone. She felt his reassuring warmth at the end of the bed. He was hers. She was just about to fall asleep when she realised that she herself had taught him none of these tricks: all had evolved from Bel himself.

12

Into this happy little Eden one day, nearly two years after Bel's arrival, came a stranger. He walked up the path and rang the bell, and when Janet came to the door he asked to see Mrs Tremorne. He was in naval uniform, small and slight, his firmly compressed mouth giving a severity to the finely-drawn, almost aesthetic face. She asked him to come in, thinking that one of Mrs Tremorne's pen friends might have materialised.

He stood in the hall, turning his cap around in his hands, yet not apparently in any nervousness for he had an air of restrained excitement and his deeply set dark blue eyes were everywhere.

'What name?' asked Janet.

'Neil MacLean,' he said then added in a soft lilting accent, 'but Mistress Tremorne will not be acquaint with it. I have been trying to trace a dog that was lost in Plymouth in 1941, and I had heard from a nurse at the hospital here that . . .' His voice trailed off: it was too long an explanation to give now, and he looked at Janet expectantly.

She could feel the blood drain out of her face, and a terrible feeling of disaster closing in. In the ten seconds that she stood silently staring at MacLean, a hundred thoughts leaped in her mind – hide Bel, deny his existence, tell this man that Mrs Tremorne was dying upstairs and couldn't be disturbed, pretend that she was a deaf mute – no she couldn't do that she had already spoken – pray that the floor would give way under him so that he could be locked for ever in the cellar with his questions about a dog that had been lost in Plymouth . . . Oh, no, oh, no . . . cried Janet's very soul, seeing the grim vista of a future that held no Bel, life, as it had been before . . .

And even as she stared at his puzzled face – for he was beginning to wonder if this strange mute woman was going to throw a fit or something – Mrs Tremorne's voice floated down the stairs. 'If that was the laundry,' she said, 'tell them that we are now missing *two* pillowcases.'

Janet found her voice. 'It is a Mr MacLean, wanting to see you about a dog,' she called up.

Mrs Tremorne was rather deaf nowadays. 'God?' she said, very puzzled, for Mr Vane, the vicar, did not usually announce himself so baldly.

'*Dog*,' shouted Janet, almost wringing her hands. '*MacLean* . . .'

Mrs Tremorne looked down and saw the dark blue uniform with some relief. She decided that he must be one of Bel's garden wall acquaintances. 'Come along up, Mr McVane,' she said pleasantly.

MacLean followed her into the small upstairs room that Alice Tremorne used nowadays so that she could watch Bel in the garden or down in the paddock with a pair of field glasses, and where this morning she had been writing to her 'children'. She hobbled across the room on swollen feet, and sat down, motioning MacLean to a seat opposite. By the arm of her chair was a small table on which lay her knitting and some photographs of Bel by a half-finished letter.

MacLean sat on the extreme edge of the chair, his face dour at the prospect of recounting the long chain of bygone fact and recent coincidence that had brought him here.

Mrs Tremorne smiled at him, 'You must be one of Bel's friends?' she said.

'I am not acquaint with the name,' said MacLean. 'As I was telling yon woman at the door, it was about a dog that

was thought to have been killed during the blitz in 1941—'
he paused, suddenly so aware of a current of hostility in this
room that he looked around, almost expecting to find someone
else, for there was no change of expression in the pale
wrinkled face opposite.

'How sad,' said Mrs Tremorne. 'So many poor animals
then—' Carefully she tidied the photographs into the letter,
then took up her knitting and turned her hooded gaze on
MacLean. She nodded with gracious sympathy. 'A terrible
time. We had no dustbins emptied or any electricity for a
week, and my garage was hit.'

'Indeed, now,' he said, as graciously, but determined to get
on with the business in hand. 'It was at the end of February,
and it's a long story, but I heard in a roundabout way that
you had acquired a dog then, one that had found you when
you were buried under your house—'

'Garage,' said Mrs Tremorne. 'It used to be the coach-
house and . . .'

'Buried under your garage—'

'In the *pit*—'

'Buried in the pit of your garage that used to be a coach-
house,' amended MacLean, softly and patiently. Their eyes
met, and he continued hurriedly, 'and I thought from what I
heard that it might well have been Ria—'

'Ria?' said Mrs Tremorne, her stumbling fingers dropping
a stitch.

"That was the name I gave him for I never knew his
real one. He was brought aboard our destroyer off St. Nazaire
with one of the survivors from the *Lancastria*. The man was
badly wounded, and I kept the dog for him. There was a
monkey too. Then I left the dog in Plymouth, and—'

'Monkey?' said Mrs Tremorne, stalling for time, time to
climb out of this bottomless pit that had so suddenly yawned
before her.

He nodded, his eyes on her hands. He had lost his initial
excitement, and felt only wary and ill at ease now, uncertain

how to confront her, uncertain even of any right, 'It was called Louis, after . . .' His voice trailed off lamely. The room was very still, only the clicking needles. Her move now . . .

Mrs Tremorne, outwardly contained, inwardly surging with a fierce determination, and entirely untroubled by conscience, decided that strategic attack was the best defence. 'The best remedy against an ill man is much ground between,' she remembered. Very well; she would set those limits now.

'And what did this dog of yours look like, my man?' she said, and the voice broke the silence with such icy deliberate condescension that MacLean's own soft voice when he answered held a tone that the one-time Ria could have interpreted for Alice Tremorne if he had been there, and would have laid his ears back in trepidation.

'Ria was not very big,' he said, 'Dark grey, with quite a thick coat, and his tail had been docked. He wasn't any breed, mind you, a terrier type, but you couldn't mistake him for his eyes – very large and bright they were. And he was the cleverest wee beast I ever came across—' Despite himself, his face had softened as he talked. 'In fact,' he confided in a sudden earnest rush, leaning forward in the chair, 'when I heard that this dog had saved someone's life, I said that will be him for sure, that will be Ria, for he had the great courage.' MacLean stopped, astonished at his loquacity.

'What a wonderful dog he must have been!' said Alice Tremorne with masterly earnestness. 'How I wish I could say the same about mine! Like so many of these overbred small poodles nowadays my darling is very timid and highly strung.'

'*Poodle?*' said MacLean.

'Poodle,' said Mrs Tremorne firmly. 'You see, I'm afraid you've wasted your time.'

Now or never. He must take this formidable old cow by the horns: 'I would like to see him,' he said.

'I'm afraid he's not here – he's with friends. *What* a pity.'

He said nothing: simply looked at her with the strange

dark blue eyes. Now she must get rid of him. Make sure he never returned.

'I am sorry about your dog,' she said, searching busily in a knitting bag for another needle to pick up a dropped stitch. 'I know how attached one can become – although I cannot understand why you did not direct your enquiries through the RSPCA. There is a very efficient branch here, as I know from my own experience – they did a wonderful job of tracing owners and findings homes for unclaimed animals. They even had a wallaby, and a three-foot python they called Daphne for a while—'

Still no response; she carried on undaunted: 'Of course it is a very long time ago, isn't it? Really a curiously long time if you were so attached to this dog? In fact,' she continued, a note of triumph creeping in, warming up to her subject with this advantage, 'one might almost think that even if the poor thing *were* still alive, and you were fortunate enough to trace it, you could hardly expect the owners to relinquish it now. Dogs cost money to feed nowadays, you know – there is little enough left over from anyone's kitchen. Now, if you would not mind, Mr McVane, I am a very busy woman—' She nodded distantly at him, as though dismissing some recalcitrant servant.

He had risen to his feet, two dark red spots of colour on his cheekbones.

'MacLean is my name,' he said, and spelled it out. 'And if it is money that counts, I would pay anything. How much would *you* be wanting for instance, Mistress Tremorne?' The scorn in the deceptively soft voice was only too apparent.

Mrs Tremorne flushed an ugly dark colour. She reached out a hand that trembled for the bell on the table. 'Go now,' she said, 'before I report you to your commanding officer for your insolence, your intrusion in my home. My companion will see you out.' Mrs Tremorne managed to convey that this would be a necessity to safeguard any valuables in his passing.

She strained towards the bell, and the ball of wool rolled off her lap and under her chair. MacLean bent down to retrieve it, but had to get on to his knees to reach under the chair. She looked down and saw a livid recent scar snaking up from behind one ear across the back of his head, the thin hair combed carefully across it. Pity and revulsion stirred simultaneously. And MacLean at that same moment, his eyes on a level with her grossly swollen feet and ankles in their gleaming buckled shoes, experienced the same reaction. He looked up at her as he handed back the wool, and she looked down, and he saw the soft creased face with the hard mouth, deep lines etched on either side, the washed-out old eyes that sparkled now, but either with pity or anger only Mrs Tremorne knew; unspokenly, like recognising like, between them a truce was called.

He stood with the ball of wool in his hand, picked up the knitting and examined it briefly, then stuck the needles through and laid it on the table.

'It is the fine sock that you are making,' he said, with only a momentary hesitation. In fact it was a terrible sock, one that to his expert eye would produce blisters in the first foot it encountered, so loosely knitted that its present gargantuan size would shrink to tiny stiff matting at the first wash. It was all that he could do to stop himself picking up the dropped stitch. He picked up his cap to give his hands something to do so that he would not be tempted.

'There are many of my socks seeing service in the navy,' said Mrs Tremorne with a kind of complacent grandeur. 'Balaclavas, scarves, mitts, too.'

MacLean had a sudden recollection of his own comments on some of the Naval Comforts that had found their way to the quartermaster's stores. 'We are always very grateful for them,' he said, pushing his mendacity to further limits.

She looked down at his own neat navy blue socks with a critical eye. 'Very nice,' she said. 'Very nicely knitted indeed. But no double heel?'

'No,' said MacLean, 'I am not liking the double heel, it is clumsy looking, yon.'

'They last *twice* as long,' said Mrs Tremorne reprovingly, 'You should ask your wife to do them that way—'

'I am not married,' said MacLean coldly, 'and I like them single – the heels that is.'

'They have to be darned,' said Mrs Tremorne, 'and what looks worse than that? Double is the *only* way.' They glared at one another.

'I never darn,' said MacLean with Olympian dignity, 'It is a foolishness. I knit new heels.' Torpedoed amidships, he thought with some satisfaction. 'This is the second pair of heels these have had,' he added, for a final salvo.

But far from going under, Mrs Tremorne was staring at his socks with admiration. '*You* knitted them?' she said. 'How wonderful – I wish I could turn heels like that – I always get a space there and have to darn it in. And a needle is such a finicky thing with these stupid hands of mine. Look,' she said, holding up the knitting, 'It's starting to form now—'

MacLean hesitated, momentarily defenceless before her admiration, then, 'Here, it's like this,' he said, and took up the sock.

Mrs Tremorne relaxed. Bel was safely in the paddock with his friend. According to his inflexible habits he would not return unless she called him from the window, or until he saw her taking her morning stroll in the garden. She would make sure nevertheless.

Janet, entering the sitting room a few minutes later at the bidding of the bell, expecting she knew not what, resigned to fetching Bel's lead and watching him limp out of her life with this sinister visitor, found the stranger on a chair drawn up close to Mrs Tremorne's, their heads bent over something.

'Now, into the back of the next stitch, careful now,' he was saying, '*Then* pass the slipped stitch over . . .'

Mrs Tremorne looked up. 'Ah, Janet, my dear,' she said. 'Coffee for two, please – oh, and Janet,' she paused meaningfully, 'if that Mr. *Bell* should call this morning, tell him to come back later – I am not to be disturbed...' MacLean's head was safely bent over the knitting. She nodded at it and one vulturish eyelid dropped.

'I'll see that he gets the message,' Janet said, almost skipping out of the door and down the stairs, heading for the paddock, her heart singing hallelujahs as she went.

'And now, Mr MacLean,' said Alice Tremorne, 'just once again – into the back of the stitch you said...' She was playing with fire, she knew; he should go now – but she could not overcome the terrible desire to speak of Bel, to hear something of his background and because of this, there was, too, the feeling of being drawn to this dour, inscrutable, little man who gave no inch to her, who had once owned Bel...

'I mind once,' he was saying, and she felt that if she had Bel's ears they would move forward now, stay pricked and intent, 'I was sitting on the deck, peaceful like, in the sun, knitting, when the *Tertian* suddenly lurched – she'd altered course to avoid a mine though I did not know it then – and the ball of wool skittered down the deck, and would have been over, but Ria, he'd skittered too, quick as a flash and he'd caught it.' Mrs Tremorne could hardly stop beaming. It was as much as she could do to refrain from capping this anecdote.

'Another time—' and MacLean was launched into a world of reminiscence. Helpless, dumb, avid for more and more, Mrs Tremorne listened, and as Bel's life at sea unfolded, so many of the missing pieces clicked into place; and something else, which she tried to push into the back of her mind and stamp upon, the unconscious laying bare of a man's life, and the gradual returning warmth to it from the coming of the dog.

'And so, you see,' he ended at last, 'that was why I left him here – I had promised Sinclair—'

Mrs Tremorne could hardly believe her ears. 'You mean to say that after all those months you deliberately *left* him?'

'Aye,' he said heavily. 'I was not wanting to – and nor was anyone else on board, for he had become part of the ship, but he was not mine, I was only minding him whiles for Sinclair.'

Mrs Tremorne's eyes were bright with battle. Any prickings of conscience she might have had were quenched forever by this appalling statement. 'You, Sinclair – pshaw!' she said, almost snorting. 'What about the *dog?* What about *his* feelings? You had him for all that time, yet you talk about this Ria as though he were a *parcel* to be re-addressed – and to someone who had only known him for hours probably, and all to honour some stupid impulsive promise! *Honour* indeed! It was pure heartlessness!' The fact that she was partly defending her own behaviour gave a passionate conviction to her words. MacLean looked troubled, she observed with pleasure.

'You don't understand,' he said at last, his words weighted with the burden of trying to explain the inexplicable debt that was owed to Ria, not just by Sinclair but by himself too. 'There was more to it than just a promise. Sinclair seemed bound to that dog – I do not know how he acquired it – for it must have followed him from France and would not give him up even in the sea. He was a strange wee dog – how he affected people. Even me—'

He stopped, looking suddenly old and defeated, but Mrs Tremorne resolutely closed her mind's eye and spoke with brisk firmness. 'At least you are talking about that poor dog in the past now,' she said, 'and I am sure that is the only sensible thing to do now. Stop blaming yourself, Mr MacLean, and lay the past to rest. It's over and done with.'

He stood up and looked out of the window across the sunny tranquil garden and paddock to the orchard beyond, his eye caught by the ambling figure of a donkey in the long grass between the apple trees. Close at its heels he could make out a small dog and some hens. He followed them until they disappeared behind a hedge.

Mrs Tremorne had stood up too. 'A beautiful view, isn't

it?' she said, and picked up MacLean's cap and handed it to him. 'It has been most interesting meeting you,' she managed to smile at him, trying to rivet his eyes safely away from the window.

'I was looking at a donkey and a dog in the field over there,' he said, and her heart missed a beat.

'What wonderful eyesight you must have,' she said smoothly. 'That is my neighbour's field.'

Donkey and dog came into sight again. MacLean's eyes narrowed intently as he watched, sudden wild hope flaring up. The dog squeezed under the gate and ran up the fence line. As he came into full view, running with an uneven gait, MacLean saw an impeccable poodle with squared off jaws and trousers, a shaven tail terminating in a knob of hair, the clipped coat a pale grey. He turned away from the window.

'I am sorry I troubled you, Mistress Tremorne,' he said wearily. 'I am owing you an apology. I will be going now.'

Before she could ring the bell he was half-way down the stairs. He let himself out. And Janet, watching him walk down the path, hurried indoors to rejoice with Mrs Tremorne.

But Mrs Tremorne was standing by the window, her face working uncontrollably, her mouth contorted in ugly grief. Janet's first thought was that she was having a heart attack, but – 'Don't stand there gaping, you dolt,' said Mrs Tremorne, 'fetch me a handkerchief.' Janet fetched two, and stood by silently while Mrs Tremorne mopped her face. 'Can you see Bel out there?' she asked at length. Bel was down there in the orchard, Janet said after a look through the field glasses, lying quietly in the sun, the darling. He must be waiting for his walkies – she would fetch Mrs Tremorne's cardigan.

I would not have done it, *I would not have done it* – I would not have lied, Mrs Tremorne told her conscience fiercely as she made her slow way into the garden; he made me do it, it was his fault, I am almost sure I would not have done it if he had not been so ruthless in his talk of promises, his *own* feelings. . . .

But Bel was untroubled by devious thought, and knew only what his senses told him. He came running now to greet this human who made up his present world, his eyes bright with love and interest. She put out her hand to him, the mesh bag with her knitting in it dangling from her wrist. He stiffened, sniffed the hand again, and now the ball of wool, the half-knitted sock – and suddenly Bel was off like a hound on a trail. Swift as an arrow up the stairs to the sitting-room, the seat, the stairs, the coffee cups, all touched briefly, and swift as an arrow down again, through the open door and along the path to the gate. And now Bel was jumping wildly at the gate, throwing himself at it, failing, falling back, throwing himself at it again. Yet he could have jumped as he usually did on to the wall, and down to the lane below; it was as though he must go through the gate, follow the reality that had gone through it already.

Janet ran to him, calling, but he took no notice, only the agonised frenzy of silent leaping and falling.

'Open the gate,' said Alice Tremorne steadily. 'Quickly, run – open the gate and let Bel go . . .

And Janet, standing by the open gate, watched the little grey shadow streak down the straight empty road until it vanished.

Half a mile away, MacLean waited at a stop for the bus that would take him back to the naval barracks at Devonport. When it had brought him here, he had felt buoyant with excitement and certainty, now he felt empty and flat – yet in a curious way expiated, and resigned. The bus drew up, the small queue shuffled forward and he swung himself on board.

'Standing room only, move along there,' said the conductress. 'Pass along there, please now – and no dogs allowed, *if* you please—' She touched MacLean's shoulder, 'Sorry, mate,' she said in a conspiratorial whisper, 'the inspector's on board—' Then in a loud cheerful voice, 'Come on, doggie—' and she smiled down.

Sitting neatly at his feet, looking up at him with the clear, dark unmistakable eyes, unblinking beneath a ludicrous top-knot secured with a red ribbon, panting slightly, but otherwise in complete control – sitting as though he had never left, was Ria. Together they got off the bus.

MacLean walked the miles back to the naval barracks and afterwards could not remember one yard of the way. Every few minutes he looked down to reassure himself of the miracle: Ria, cool, contained and undemonstrative to him as ever, trotting at his heels with the slight limp to which he had not yet become accustomed. He paused only once as they neared the dockyard gates, and removed the red ribbon.

Exactly three days later, at ten o'clock in the morning, Bel returned to The Cedars. Janet heard him at the garden gate, and ran to let him in. He took the stairs in three bounds, pushed open the bedroom door, and jumped on to Mrs Tremorne's bed. Mrs Tremorne had been gazing blankly down into the unresponsive depths of a cup of cold tea, willing herself to get up and face a day that lacked any incentive for getting up.

She was possibly the happiest woman in England the following moment, with Janet a close second, while Bel in his excitement made the first clumsy movement of his life and upset the cup of tea. The dog Ria might be undemonstrative, cool and contained; Mrs Tremorne knew only a Bel who openly and enthusiastically demonstrated his affection for her, but even she had never seen this Bel who nudged at her face with his muzzle as though he could not get close enough, who pawed at her forearm, and made whining singing noises. Janet and Alice Tremorne wept unashamedly together.

After that Bel followed his usual morning routine as though he had never been absent. When the faint chink and rattle of the impending vacuuming session was heard downstairs, and Mrs Tremorne was getting dressed, he padded downstairs, looked in the kitchen, found no familiar water bowl, or even his plate upon which normally reposed at this hour his ten o'clock offering – a biscuit or square of chocolate from her precious sweet ration. He sat in the kitchen entrance now, gazing earnestly at Janet, a faint air of reproof in his manner; and so compelling was his gaze that it was not long before she interpreted it to his satisfaction, giving him, in heartfelt gratitude, her entire ration for the week.

As though hypnotised, she followed him, again through custom, and opened the front door. Bel trotted briskly down the path towards the orchard, checked on the welcoming hens, and followed by his flock continued on to the paddock. The old donkey broke into a trot towards him and then a canter. Bel ran towards him and sailed through the air to land on the dusty brown back. It was as though he had never gone. The only difference in him was that he no longer wore a ribbon; and someone had clipped the long hair on the top of his head.

He was there when Mrs Tremorne made her slow way to the orchard. They had their lunch there, the three of them, and afterwards Bel accompanied the old lady up to her room for her afternoon rest, and had a good sleep himself, under the pink eiderdown.

At four o'clock, after a pleasant tea, before which he balanced biscuits on his nose, retrieved his ball and gave it back to Janet to throw again, Bel indicated that he had business elsewhere; he sat by the door and then, when let out, sat before the gate in silent supplication, again ignoring the easy access over the wall. Janet looked up at Mrs Tremorne who watched from the upstairs window. This time she seemed almost happy.

'Yes, open it,' she called down; and then had an inspiration, for, apart from MacLean's name and rank she had no idea where he was stationed, or how to get in touch with him. 'Tie on a fresh ribbon before he goes,' she said. But the hair

173

was too short, and the ribbon had to be tied to his collar. He ran off without a backward glance.

So Ria, arriving back at Devonport barracks three quarters of an hour later, was able to inform MacLean how and where Bel had spent the afternoon.

13

Now Bel and Ria merged into Bel Ria, a composed purposeful little figure who was often to be seen on the back roads between Devonport and The Cedars, trotting along in his uneven but fast gait, looking neither to left nor to right, undiverted by other dogs, even interesting smells, intent only on reaching his alternative world. On reaching The Cedars he behaved as Bel; on returning to Devonport he was MacLean's undemonstrative Ria.

Communication was soon established between his two owners. Mrs Tremorne tied a label on his collar with an invitation to tea. The deft-fingered MacLean fashioned a small permanent waterproof capsule into which he rolled his acceptance.

It was at first a stiff, very formal tea party, with both sides wary, but by some tacit understanding no mention was made – and never was – of their first meeting. Guilt was as unfamiliar an emotion to Alice Tremorne as triumph was to Neil MacLean, but disquietude was now mutual: the spectre of a third and rightful owner – rightful to MacLean anyway, but to be fought to the last inch by Mrs Tremorne – hovered uneasily and unspoken between them. This drew them unwillingly closer together. Besides, there was so much that Mrs Tremorne wanted to know that only MacLean could unfold. By the end of the meal he was winding a ball of wool for her, and having learned that sultanas and itinerant knife grinders were now unavailable had indicated that he might be able to remedy this lack.

Throughout, Bel Ria sat between them, his eyes as always going from one face to the other as though following the conversation, relieved when rapport was reached, clearly anxious when it was restrained. When, to MacLean's barely concealed disapproval, his customary saucer of milky tea and sugar was handed down, he handled the situation with an almost uncanny perception; cocking one eye and ear briefly in MacLean's direction, hesitating only fractionally, he lapped his tea, then lay quietly down and closed his eyes – thus tactfully omitting his usual sitting up to beg and saluting routine, always followed by a comfortable session on Mrs Tremorne's lap.

Acquaintance gradually flowered with Bel Ria as courier for messages and observations and, as MacLean's talent for fixing things around the house was revealed, urgent enquiries about what to do with a leaking U-bend or a Hoover emitting alarming sparks, followed. On receiving one of these SOSs, MacLean would arrive as soon as he had time off and put things right. Once he turned up with a pair of overalls in his gas mask haversack, then armed with a saw and bucket of tar, he 'sorted', as he described the operation, the apple trees. Shortly after he took over the grass cutting, for the gardener could only spare an hour or so a week now and the garden was beginning to look like a wilderness. From there it was but a short step to clearing choked gutters and drains and a coat of wood preservative on the henhouse. At first he had little to say; he would do whatever he considered had to be done and then depart, brushing aside any thanks, and refusing always to stay for any meals. It was as though he could not again bear to see his Ria of the Ark behaving as the pampered Bel of The Cedars.

Alice Tremorne taxed him with this one day, and he admitted it bluntly: he didn't like dogs – or any animals for that matter – made fools of with tricks and the like. She was silent for a moment. Her colour was high and she looked angry; but when she spoke at last there was no sharpness in her voice, only a new almost weary tone that MacLean had not heard before.

'I don't think it is we who make fools of dogs,' she said slowly. 'I am beginning to think that they make fools of us – they show up our needs and weaknesses somehow.' As though embarrassed by this insight she handed him a glass of her Elderberry '38 to try. She knew now that he was not the ghostly X of her jealousy. Ria could never have danced for this man.

MacLean sipped in silence, looking thoughtful, but whether he was considering the bouquet or her words she was not to know.

'Aye,' he said at last, the word that she recognised by now did not necessarily mean assent, but was merely a useful non-committal. They were standing by the window upstairs, looking down and across the garden to the roofless shell of the coach-house. 'Yon needs sorting,' he said, with a disapproving scowl in its direction.

'Impossible!' said Mrs Tremorne. 'This dreadful war – carpenters nowadays are either so doddery that they'd fall off the first rung of a ladder or charging so much that it would be out of the question.'

'Indeed now!' said MacLean, his face brightening in a way that she had also come to recognise presaged the taking-up of a challenge, or the setting in order of the disorderly. Her potting shed for example was now an uncobwebbed and regimented delight.

He left shortly afterwards, as abruptly and brusquely as ever, and she watched him walk down the drive to the gate, her heart turning over as always at the sight of her darling Bel following him, however temporarily, out of her life. 'Half a loaf was better than none,' Janet had consoled with maddening logic. Indeed it was – nevertheless she still found herself longing that MacLean might be transferred to some remote, dog-debarred posting, and his half restored to her in whole impeccable poodledom once more, his lovely silken topknot unsnipped. . . .

(There had been bitter argument over Bel Ria's appearance. She was proud of her grooming talent, and the combing and brushing had been a pleasurable daily routine, but Mac-Lean had wanted a reversal to the shaggy naval look, claiming stubbornly that he would look a proper twit followed by a poodle with a hair ribbon at the barracks. In the end a compromise had been reached, engineered by the diplomatic Janet: why not let his coat grow out all over, but then keep it short to something like Bedlington terrier length? Both had grudgingly accepted this, both had secretly admired the compact result; and both had suffered the same short stab of realisation when they saw that a few white hairs had grown in to lightly brindle the short curly coat.)

She knew that he had a fortnight's leave coming up, and the thought of the consequent total separation was unbearable. Yet deep down, she had to admit that she would miss this dour little man's unannounced visits, miss his forthrightness, the challenge of his uncompromising attitude towards her. And so would Janet, she thought with sudden amusement: there were times nowadays when she was positively skittish.

He took her unawares therefore on his next appearance when he put forward a proposal, to which he had obviously given considerable thought, and which was presented with much delicate celtic circumvention to preserve his own deeply-rooted sense of what was a fitting distance between them. Alice Tremorne was given to understand that it might be a very good idea if he were to spend his leave restoring the coach-house. Admittedly he wasn't a carpenter or a bricklayer but it was possible that he could overcome this handicap, and he knew a chippie chap who was the great one for fixing things and would know where to lay hands on some timber and tools. 'Some things are better done through the likes of him,' he said with a vagueness that she thought it better not to question.

She was delighted. Providence had smiled upon her again, and this time the alligator bag would see to it that the smile remained, for surely, she reasoned to herself, this was a business proposition? Already she was organising the details in her mind, and out they came now in a fulsome rush: Janet would turn the Yellow Bedroom into a bed-sitting-room for Mr MacLean's leave – it was such a sunny room, and he would be very comfortable there – and of course it must be a proper financial arrangement with the proper going wage ... On she went without interruption until suddenly she became aware of a coolness in the atmosphere. Bel Ria, sitting beside her, laid the weather vanes of his ears back and looked covertly around.

When MacLean spoke his voice was very cold indeed. There would be no financial arrangement; he would be doing it because he chose to do it. There would be no bed-sitting-room in the house, however yellow, however comfortable. The harness room was still weather-proof, there was water from the pump there, a fireplace to cook by – 'and the lavatory still works,' he finished with steely finality. If Mistress Tremorne would supply a camp bed and a few cooking utensils, that would be all he would be needing.

But Mistress Tremorne could not and would not countenance such a one-sided makeshift arrangement. They set to, hammer and tongs, into an argument closely followed by the worried ears and eyes of Bel Ria between them. At the height of it he suddenly yawned hugely, rose, stretched and departed downstairs to Janet, leaving behind a disconcerted lull in the battle.

Unexpectedly, Alice Tremorne was seized with a witchlike cackling of laughter. 'He's right,' she managed to say at last. 'We *are* being very boring indeed – I give in! Now will you give in over your idea of crouching over a grate with a frying pan and do me one more favour – accept our hospitality for meals?'

MacLean could make concessions too. He accepted gracefully, even managing to restore Mrs Tremorne to the position of benefactor.

'It's the grand holiday you will be giving me,' he said. 'Board and lodging and recreation – what more could I want? I had nowhere else to go anyway – except perhaps to Scotland, to sort things out with Donald Sinclair—'

The words hung between them. Alice Tremorne interpreted correctly. 'That can wait,' she said flatly. 'It will wait for ever as far as I am concerned. But the coach-house needs sorting out now before the winter, doesn't it? And, after all, I am a very old lady with no one to turn to for help with it, aren't I?'

She managed to sound tremulous and pathetic.

'Aye,' said MacLean, enigmatically as ever. He patted Bel Ria, something she had never seen him do before, and nodded cheerfully enough as he departed, but his eyes looked troubled.

Mrs Tremorne watched him go with the stirrings of real affection. Already she was planning that she would feed him like a fighting cock during his stay, even if it meant exploring the murkier depths of the black market, for apart from that being the only way she could repay him, he looked as though he needed building-up. He was far too thin, and often seemed tired and strained. Perhaps it was because of that terrible scar on his head. Somehow she must break down his reserve and get him to talk about the days of the destroyer and get him to fill in the past. She plotted happily.

He came with an ecstatically returning Bel Ria in that glorious portentuous autumn of 1943. He settled into the tackroom – finding that Janet had determinedly added her own touches of a carpet, reading light, and even curtains at the windows – and as he took off his uniform in exchange for working rig, he shed all worries and the outside world of war for the little self-contained one of The Cedars.

The sirens still wailed their nightly dirge across the land to the approaching bombers. Rationing was even tighter, commodities were exhausted and making-do had become an inventive commonplace, but certain hope was abroad now, growing daily stronger as the pressure of the Allies mounted in every theatre of war; from North Africa to Russia; from Italy today to Burma tomorrow – to the certain dawn of that day when the great combined strength would leave these shores and return to France for the final reckoning.

Against this mighty background were set the victories and defeats of The Cedars – and countless other Cedars across the country. The triumphal bonus of a pound of offal against the surrender of the Italian fleet; fireless grates and the tedium of the blackout against the conditions of the Murmansk convoys; the claustrophobia and damp of the air raid shelter against a midget submarine in a Norwegian fjord – or the restoration of a coach-house against the homeless havoc left in the wake of bombers. Yet all the apparently minuscule trivia, the grumblings, the inconsequential pleasures, were woven into the background of the global tapestry of war. Alice Tremorne's equal indignation with the laundry, and Hitler, the quality of sausages and the Emperor of Japan; Janet Carpenter's pleasure in the underwear potential of half a German parachute; Neil MacLean's problems with his conscience, roof measurements and blistered palms – all these were there. Even the way a little dog's coat was shorn to the winds of compromise was a part of the fabric of that time.

Bel Ria's reaction to his seperate lives brought together virtually under the same roof was unpredictable: he was plainly very put out at first. Although he slept in Alice Tremorne's bedroom, walked with MacLean across the fields in the evening, and sat between them at meals, during the rest of the day he paid frequent restless visits from one to another and seemed displaced and unable to relax with either, as though the fusion of his dual roles bewildered him. It took him a day or two to adjust to the situation. Or perhaps, his allegiance no longer divided, he felt free to pursue his own ends, for he took to spending more time with the donkey and with Janet

– their company undoubtedly restful and undemanding, for neither expected anything of him other than what he was, and Janet was not above a down-to-earth scolding if he left muddy paw prints on the floor or rolled luxuriously on the compost heap. He spent many more hours too on his garden wall vigil, his eyes distant, yet his ears flicking to all movement up and down the road.

'It's as though he were watching for someone to come up that road – I used to think it was whoever he belonged to before, but you are here now – and he still waits,' said Mrs Tremorne one morning. She was sitting in a garden chair by a neat pile of stacked timber, pressed into dating and listing the intact wine bottles which MacLean had excavated from the debris. Yesterday he had found the shoes that had been blown off her feet nearly two and a half years ago: side by side, the toes turned slightly out as their owner had left them, they had come to light under a pile of lathes. Now he paused in his hammering and emptied his mouth of nails.

'He would lie like that for hours on board too,' he said. 'Staring at nothing, as though he was sleeping with his eyes open. Hyacinthe used to curl up beside him whiles and it seemed he never even noticed she was there.'

Alice Tremorne put down her dusters and produced two bottles of beer and two glasses from her bag like rabbits from a conjurer's hat. 'Tell me about her, Neil,' she said persuasively, eager as a child for the next installment of a story, one of which she could never have enough. 'And about Barkis, and the monkey – Luigi, wasn't it?'

'Louis,' he said. 'Poor wee Louis –' he broke off abruptly, and poured the beer. Plainly he didn't want to think about the monkey now. 'You should not be stopping me at my work,' he said with reproving frown.

'You need a break,' said Alice Tremorne, 'Oh, come along now, Neil – tell me about the ship's cat,' she cajoled.

So he told her about Hyacinthe, about her majestic ways and six toes to each front paw, her apparent ability to receive and decipher signals with the antennae of her unusually long whiskers so that she never missed a sailing, always managing to get back on board in the nick of time however solicitous the attentions of her current Lothario on shore. 'A real "pier-head jumper" she was,' he said.

And he told her something of that terrible dawn on their way back from Tobruk when two JU 88s swooped out of the rising sun to sink one of their three destroyers and leave *Tertian* lying low in the water, mortally wounded from two direct hits. Some passing hand had picked up Hyacinthe where she lay in the scuppers with both front legs broken, and dropped her on a stretcher being passed across to the last destroyer alongside. How Hyacinthe had got back to Alexandria with the rest of *Tertian*'s survivors and had been taken to hospital with them. And how a Surgeon Captain, an orthopaedic specialist in civilian life, had set her legs in a plaster jacket that left her head sticking out of one end, and her hindquarters and tail out of the other.

'Then,' said MacLean, smiling down at Bel Ria who had forsaken the wall to join them and sat listening as apparently spellbound as Mrs Tremorne, 'then one of the crew bored a hole through the plaster sleeves, just below the paws, to take an axle for two rubber-tyred wheels and turned her into a kind of self-propelling trolley. She used to wheel herself around the hospital, still managing to look dignified despite that contrivance, her tail straight up in the air like a flue brush, and everyone signed her cast, even the Surgeon Rear Admiral.'

She had made a perfect recovery, her fame had swept even further abroad; and then there had been much rivalry about her future, for it seemed that everyone coveted the stately Hyacinthe: the hospital staff put forward a strong claim, there had been a well laid plot for cat-napping hatched below a cruiser's decks, and it was even rumoured that the C-in-C Mediterranean Fleet had designs upon her. In the end she went to a mine layer.

'Until that was sunk on the Tobruk run too,' said MacLean.

'But yon cat still had plenty of lives. She survived that, swimming like an otter for a float, their SBA told me, and I heard later that she came back to England – in a submarine of all things.'

'What a pity she can't write a book about her experiences,' said Mrs Tremorne.

'If she could, I'm thinking that it would be banned,' said MacLean with a pawky smile. 'She was a proper sailor with a husband in every port.'

'And Barkis? You haven't told me yet what happened to him?' asked Mrs Tremorne, aware of Bel Ria's sudden quivering interest as she spoke the name.

'The bridge received a direct hit,' said MacLean, so tersely that she forebore to ask any further questions.

He did not tell her then, or ever, of the ghastly shattered shambles that had been the bridge, of the scalding screaming horror of the engine room, or the twisted tangles of metal mangling the bodies of his shipmates. Of Reid. Of Lessing. Or of any of those sixty-eight shipmates who went down with *Tertian.* Nor did he tell her then of his last sight of Louis that still haunted him in its lonely bravura . . .

He went off to get a ladder. Mrs Tremorne was unable to resist the temptation: 'Barkis –' she said softly to Bel Ria, '*Hyacinthe, Louis*—' but almost immediately was filled with shame for his eyes searched hers eagerly as she spoke their names, then he turned and looked back down the garden as though expecting them to materialise. She felt very small. To distract him, she forced herself to take the now increasingly painful walk to the paddock and the donkey.

'Walkies, my darling,' she said. 'Fetch my stick – fetch Missus's garden stick. We'll go and see how Fred is.'

Neil MacLean sawed and hammered and painted the days away, completely absorbed in his work. The first two days, palms blistered, back aching and head throbbing, he had fallen into his camp bed in the tack room almost immediately after supper. Now, brown and fit, free for the first time in months of the headaches which had plagued him since they removed the fragment of metal from his head in the hospital at Alexandria, he did full justice to Mrs Tremorne's carefully plotted meals. Armed with the extra rationing points provided for HM Forces on leave, she excelled herself.

Neil, as she and Janet always called him now, had developed an easy relationship with her, never deferring, often blunt, yet always maintaining a balance of diffidence. Her ruthless determination amused him; his stubborness exasperated and challenged her. Both loved an argument, and they had much to argue about, for both had hard and fast opinions about almost everything. But disagreement always discomforted Bel Ria, and his initial nervous yawnings, heralding his imminent condemnatory departure from the scene, were usually enough to make them agree to differ on the subject. Mrs Tremorne took to using the diplomatic all embracing 'Aye' as well. So did Janet, but teasingly.

Janet had blossomed, and her refreshing down-to-earth viewpoint, her often hilarious gossiping anecdotes, were the perfect foil to his taciturnity. He found time to refurbish an old bicycle discovered rusting in the toolshed for her shopping expeditions, and he found too that she made an excellent apprentice, with a good head for heights. Followed up the ladder by the familiarly nimble paws of a delighted Bel Ria, they spent many hours working companionably on the roof. Once Mrs Tremorne had got over her fears and realised that her darling was as at home on a ladder as on the staircase, she relaxed and watched progress benignly through her field glasses.

Sometimes, a formidable opponent, she played chess in the evenings with Neil. Sometimes they read or listened to the wireless; sometimes all three sat knitting or sewing, Bel Ria asleep in their contented midst. But Mrs Tremorne liked it best when she could persuade Neil to talk about the days of *Tertian*.

One evening he brought over a few photographs to show

her. The first was of a fair haired young man, his eyes squinting against a low sun. He stood by a ship's rail, wearing a duffle coat, a small monkey muffled up in a rollnecked jersey in his arms, and by his feet, looking up at the monkey, was Ria of *Tertian*, far sturdier then in his thick almost shaggy coat but still recognisably her Bel.

'Atlantic convoy,' said MacLean. 'That was the doctor. He wasn't long qualified, but I served under none better. He sent me these pictures after I got back here.'

The second was of a thick-set bearded man in tropical uniform, one hand half-raised in salute, newly stepped off a gangway, at his heels a massive bull terrier looking towards the camera with a pleased shark-like smile of recognition.

'The Captain coming aboard at Gib. with Barkis,' said MacLean. 'Himself was the fine gentleman,' he added with such finite simplicity that Alice Tremorne passed swiftly on to the last picture.

This was of a very tall young seaman with the same little monkey perched on his shoulder, this time wearing a shoulder harness and lead over a white singlet and a pair of absurd white shorts.

'Lessing and Louis in the Mediterranean,' said MacLean.

Mrs Tremorne seemed fascinated by the photograph, looking at it under the light with a magnifying glass. 'So tiny and delicate,' she marvelled. 'Such a little scrap of a thing to have gone through so much—'

'He was a thrawn wee beast,' said MacLean with some vehemence. 'At least with me,' he added with sudden honest insight, 'as if he knew I couldn't abide his capers, but the men were daft about him, and so was Ria for that matter. When Ria didn't come back after Plymouth, he was aye searching for him on board. For a while he wouldn't eat, and he was all huddled up and listless, the way sick monkeys are, but it was warm in the Med, and there was plenty of fruit and nuts and the like, and after a while he seemed to forget and settled down.'

'And where is he now?' asked Mrs Tremorne.

'He went with our Ark,' said MacLean, his face expressionless.

Mrs Tremorne had not heard properly. '*Where* did you say?' she repeated.

MacLean looked across at her. She was looking down at the photograph, her face soft. Ria watched him, his eyes uneasy. 'He went with Lessing and the others—' he said gently, 'and he's still with them, still the same.'

'What a happy ending,' said Mrs Tremorne with relief.

'Aye,' said MacLean, and got out the chess board.

He thought of Louis again that night, lying awake in the tack room that now looked as neat and snug and ship-shape as he could have wished. He had had no affection or sentiment for the animal, but his end had been such a lonely one and its defiant rejection had affected him profoundly.

In those desperate moments after *Tertian* had been hit, there was naturally no time to think of Louis. Helplessly out of commission, *Tertian* was a sitting target. The decision was taken to abandon ship, then sink her themselves. Their sister ship, *Trumpeter*, now moving in alongside, was an even more vital target with her decks already crammed with *Tertian*'s survivors, and every minute counted. In the last moments, all hands had turned to in searching out the wounded.

One of the last to leave, scrambling over the wreckage, the coxswain saw a flicker of movement among it and Louis leaped on to the rail ahead. The coxswain grabbed as he passed but Louis struggled and bit and fought free to swarm up a stay out of reach.

Trumpeter stood off and trained her guns, while on her packed decks the small company of *Tertian*'s survivors were the silent shocked spectators. Close to MacLean, the quartermaster watching through binoculars spotted Louis just before the first salvo. High on the wireless mast that still remained miraculously straight and intact, he clung to a stay, his yellow duster trailing from one paw. His head was turned in the direction of *Trumpeter*. The guns thundered.

He was glad now that he had substituted the satisfactory ambiguity to Alice Tremorne, for he had not realised until he saw her with the photograph that she had such a vulnerable core. Why burden her with something that had tormented him enough in the sick feverish activity of his mind for weeks afterwards, when twisting restlessly in the hot unreality of the long hospital nights, there had been plenty of time to think, to try and equate his obsession over the manner of death of one capuchin monkey with the deaths of so many fine men.

Thinking back to that time from the serenity of his mind tonight, it was as though he saw it in perspective for the first time and was able to understand at last: Louis had been the only alien, the only one out of his element against that background. Loss of life was an accepted gamble that men took when they went to war. But no animal went to war: caught up in man's lethal affairs, they were an irreconcilable aberration.

He suddenly recalled the soldier's ravings about bears and horses and rabbits – the 'innocents' he had called them. The innocents? Fanciful talk he would have said then – ravings indeed. But now? All he knew now was that nothing could ever be the same again; he could never return to the laboratory after the war – there would be too many Louis' and Rias and Hyacinthes there to remind him.

He slept, absolved, the little ghost of Louis laid to rest at last, along with all the other animals that had passed through his hands, as innocent now as them.

Early in the morning, as though to rid his conscience entirely of the last thing that remained on it, he wrote a long letter to Donald Sinclair, the first communication since that stark telegram from Plymouth. He ended it:

. . . so that you must tell me what you would like done for I am not easy in my mind to bide this way when it is your right. I should have written long before. Mind you I do

188

not speak for Mrs Tremorne – after all this time she thinks of the dog as hers, and in a way this is so – if it was not for her this letter would not need to be written. She has been willing enough to let him be with me this half and half way, but only because she would do anything for him and it seemed to be his own decision. He is a strange dog.

I will hope to hear from you soon. In the meantime I will try and make him stay here when my leave is up, for finding his own way between D'port and here is too risky with the traffic. And too long, as I am thinking now that he is nearer eleven than ten.

He addressed and sealed the envelope, then stamped it resolutely. He would post it now, before breakfast, before he had any second thoughts. . . . There was a faint scratch at the door: Bel Ria had arrived, unusually early, in time to accompany him. He limped more noticeably than usual on their way to the postbox, sometimes going on three legs.

It would rain before the afternoon, said Alice Tremorne sagely – her own aching joints had foretold this as well this morning. She was half way down the stairs when she made her pronouncement, making difficult progress. Near the bottom she stumbled and almost fell. She waved Neil imperiously aside when he went forward to take her arm, but he took it anyway and to divert her fumings as he helped her across the hall to the windowseat, he told of his decision to leave Bel Ria when his leave ended. The news was not received with the pleasure he had expected. He could feel her arm beneath his become suddenly rigid, and for a moment she seemed quite stunned.

'Does that mean that . . . that you are going away, going back to sea?' she said at last, and far from sounding exultant, she sounded almost fearful.

'Nothing of the kind,' he said, surprised, 'I'll be at Devonport for a while yet, I hope. It just seemed that with the winter coming on it would be easier for him.' He felt her relax.

She sat down, but before she turned her head away he saw to his embarrassment that she had tears in her eyes. 'Mind you, Mistress Tremorne,' he went on severely, 'that doesn't mean any fancy work with the clippers and ribbons and the like the moment I've gone – there's plenty to be done yet outside so I'll be be backwards and forwards to keep an eye on him.'

'But perhaps he won't stay once you've gone through that gate,' said Mrs Tremorne worriedly. A few drops of rain splashed on the window, and she recovered herself. 'You see,' she said triumphantly, 'it's going to pour!' Then, with sudden Machiavellian cunning, she went on: 'Why don't you take Janet to the pictures this afternoon for a start? To get him used to the idea that you *will* come back?'

'The *pictures?* In the *afternoon?*' he said, so obviously horrified at such decadence that she laughed.

'*Goodbye Mr Chips* is hardly an orgy. Bel and I will have a nice afternoon pampering ourselves in front of the fire. Why don't you go?'

'Why not? Why not indeed?' he said with sudden reckless decision. 'I might do just that—'

Mrs Tremorne watched them go. Bel Ria made no attempt to follow. 'How *nice*,' she said as she settled down for a cosy chat with him on her lap, 'How nice it would be – I could bring my bedroom downstairs, which would be much easier for us, wouldn't it? – and they could have the whole of the upstairs, and then we could all be together! Wouldn't that be lovely, my darling?' Bel Ria regarded her with enthusiastic interest. After a while they both had a little nap.

When she woke up she confided another thought: 'The coach-house would make a wonderful surgery, wouldn't it?' Bel Ria looked at her enquiringly. 'I mean if he went back and finished his veterinary degree one day – did you know he only had a year to go?' He stirred his tail agreeably. The rain drummed on the windows. It was very peaceful. They had another little nap.

Bel Ria seemed reassured when he saw that Neil's work

clothes remained in the tack room on the day of his departure. Janet held him at the gate, subdued but unprotesting as she waved his paw cheerfully in farewell. Then he followed her quite happily to find Fred and the morning's egg harvest.

Donald Sinclair's reply, awaiting at the barracks, was movingly warm and percipient:

> ... besides, I have no 'right' as you said in your letter – it is between you and Mrs Tremorne, for the dog has belonged to both of you over these years, and he was with me for less than 24 hours. It was a queer time too, the more I think about it – if the dog had never found me in that ditch in France everything would have been different. And his real owner might still be alive. That woman risked everything for me, and in the end the only way I could repay her at all was to see that her dog was cared for – and that was where you came in.
>
> I hope that one day we will meet and have a good yarn about those days – perhaps next year when I expect to come south for a week or so ...

There was a PS: 'Re-reading your letter I think that you have answered it yourself already! I think that she would be well content with your decision.'

Neil handed the letter to Mrs Tremorne on his next visit without comment.

When she had finished reading she was silent for a long time.

'So it was a woman,' she said slowly at last. 'The one he really belonged to, I mean—' When she spoke again, she sounded almost sad, 'I think I always knew that he never really belonged to either of us, he's just a part of both of us. Look at him—' she went on, glancing across the room to where Bel Ria lay in a patch of sunlight, 'you see, he isn't the shaggy Ria of your photographs, or the almost-poodle Bel of mine. He's *Bel Ria* and he became that between us.'

MacLean could only nod. She looked at the letter again

then handed it back. 'Strange – how he *found* people, first Sinclair, and then me. But not you—'

He put the letter back in his pocket with an air of finality. 'Perhaps he found me out instead—' he said briskly. 'And now, I've got until six, so there's just time to get another coat of paint on before the light goes.' Clearly the matter was closed.

Seconds before he had uttered the words, the seemingly fast asleep Bel Ria had risen, stretched, and made for the door where he now stood looking back expectantly, his tail stirring slowly.

14

The question of possession had been dispelled and was never to be revived. Bel Ria was left to himself as the humans in his life became increasingly possessed by their own intertwining lives, but so gradually did this detachment come about over the following year that it went unremarked. The extended solitude on the wall, the longer withdrawals into sleep in their company were taken for a natural quietude in his undisputed security.

Only occasionally now did he search their faces to interpret some shadow of expression, or sit alertly with his head turning from one to another as they spoke. It was as though he had mastered their communication and that there was nothing further to learn. Yet in other ways he appeared to have drawn closer, for the deeply ingrained need of his character and training to give of himself drove him to become even more prescient to their actions or wishes. Almost before an idea had been formed – such as going out for a walk or wondering where he was – he would appear with eager questioning eyes, as though he had already received the summons and waited only to learn their requirements of him. Always minutes before Neil's or Janet's arrival he would be watching from the window or the wall, and the enthusiasm of his greeting grew more demanding.

He performed his day to day tricks for Mrs Tremorne more insistently, prolonging the session whenever possible, even adding to them. But the impulse to bestow his dance seldom overtook him now, for he was no longer rewarded with her pleasure, only frustrated by her concern. It had seemed to her that he had become over-intense and anxious then, and sometimes he even panted as though the performance exacted too great an effort, and because of this, sympathetically attributing it to his rheumatism in the injured paw, she tried to avoid it altogether.

Even Neil, returning after a long period of absence in the spring of 1944 noticed no change other than a muzzle more greyed than he remembered, although this lack of awareness was hardly surprising that day as his mind's eye was almost fully occupied with more pressing affairs. He had been posted to a Combined Operations base on the south coast and had come back on an unexpected forty-eight hour leave.

Bel Ria had anticipated his coming from his post on the wall since early morning, and had shadowed him from the moment he had turned in at the gate, but after the first greeting it was Janet who received all the attention from then on, for within half an hour of his arrival she and Neil had become engaged.

Janet had made only one proviso: that Alice Tremorne should always be their responsibility, no matter what. Neil seemed only surprised that she would bother to mention this.

'But I've never thought other than that I'd be taking on the pair of you,' he said. 'Do you want me to propose to her as well?'

'It won't always be easy,' Janet warned. 'You don't know what it was like before. Bel Ria can't live for ever, and when he's gone she'll be lost for something to lavish her love and attention on. You're *sure* you want to take it on? And please, no "aye" for an answer this time.'

At his feet Bel Ria looked up. Neil's mind suddenly went back to the same discomforting intensity in the inflamed eyes of a small black oil-reeking dog by the head of a stretcher, awaiting his answer then as now.

194

'There will be bairns to take his place one day,' he said abruptly. 'And yes, I was never surer of anything.'

He bent down to pat Bel Ria and then, to Janet's amazement, picked him up and held him in his arms. Bel Ria managed to look so awkward and embarrassed by this departure from custom that he put him down after a moment.

'I've never seen you do that before,' she said.

'I was just seeing what it felt like,' he said sheepishly.

Everthing would go on just the same, they agreed as they walked back to the house, until Neil was demobbed and would get his gratuity – perhaps even a grant as well – to finish off the year for a veterinary degree. And in the meantime, as Mrs Tremorne's bedroom had been moved downstairs to the dining-room, perhaps they would be able to use part of the upstairs as their own quarters. And . . .

From the window Alice Tremorne saw them coming, Bel Ria running ahead, the three beings who filled her life. She sat back in her chair with a deep sigh of content. Bel Ria had not been alone in his precognition. He arrived now, well ahead of the others, and displaced *The Times* in her lap. She hugged him tightly, and then in her excitement dabbed her eyes with one of his ears instead of her handkerchief. 'At *last* – I was beginning to think we'd have to do it for him!' she said. He scratched the ear absently, then examined his paw as though he had never seen it before, so she went on with his answer: 'So nice – so *exactly* right!'

A few minutes later, she received the news with every appearance of overjoyed astonishment. Not long afterwards she had a sudden inspiration for the separate conversion of the upstairs part of the house. They received this with equal pleasure and surprise.

(However, the seeds of the coach-house/surgery plan could wait for a while yet to be planted, she decided to herself after lunch; there was still this tedious war to be won. Doggedly she cast on the stitches for her twenty-seventh balaclava.)

In June, immediately following D-Day, as her part in the

all-out determination of those at home to back up the invading armies in France, Janet took on a part-time post with the ARP in addition to the railway canteen, so Mrs Tremorne and Bel Ria were alone for most of the day now.

But far from being lonely they were very content and occupied, and each had the other's undivided attention. Wine-making now impossible – even to Alice Tremorne – with rationed sugar, they had taken up the challenge of cooking. Planting high stools in strategic resting places around the kitchen and scullery, she moved from one to another, talking to her keenly interested supervisor and taster ensconced at table level on a nearby chair, as she put her full ingenuity into the test of making something delicious out of the nothing of war-time substitutes and those rewarding eggs. The results were greatly appreciated by the still steady stream of visiting members of the Forces.

The months slipped by most satisfyingly. In August the re-entry into Paris was celebrated with *Oeufs parisiens;* in September a landmine exploding in a field half a mile away rocked the house and flattened a magnificent *Soufflé Arnhem;* October brought the occupation of Athens and exotic (curried) *Oeufs à la greque.* Even the hens were doing their bit. Her triumph was the wedding feast with one of them in aspic.

After this excitement Neil returned to Sussex to his stone frigate posting, Janet to her jobs, and Bel Ria and Mrs Tremorne settled down again, finding contentment even in the winter's cold and fuel shortages for they avoided these by moving almost permanently into the warm cosiness of the kitchen, with armchairs, footrests, wireless and all.

Bel Ria seemed very content with this tranquil, undemand-ing kitchen existence, becoming reluctant even to desert the warmth of the fire for the wall, or the company of Fred and the hens. Too content altogether, Mrs Tremorne decided, noticing that he stretched himself rather stiffly nowadays be-fore making one of his briefer and briefer necessary sorties into the garden.

'This will never do,' she told him briskly one cold February morning when he poked his nose out of the door, withdrew it swiftly before the icy blast, and returned to the kitchen. 'We're becoming soft – anyone would think we're getting old,' and she began to coax and scold him from his bed by the fire for longer and longer periods. Out they went, rain or shine, wind or frost.

'If *I* can do it – *you* can!' she told him mercilessly as they limped along together in the thin cold sunshine one day. 'Smell that—' she commanded, poking the rich earth with her cane, 'and *that*—' as she prodded a primrose clump. And 'Fetch!' she exhorted as she whacked at rotting windfalls and fir cones – until suddenly the reluctant exercise turned into an exuberant, rolling, snuffing, digging discovery in the irresistible challenge of spring. Very soon Bel Ria had forsaken the hearthside and was back in charge of his vibrant garden domain.

It was not until the day of Victory in Europe that she was forced to admit in her heart that he was slowing up. Out in the garden to share in the jubilation of the long silenced bells pealing across the countryside, she saw Bel Ria try and fail to make the low jump on to the wall.

'Perhaps we're not *quite* as young as we were, my loved one,' she admitted, 'but let's rejoice anyway!' and she called in two youngsters passing by to move a garden seat close to the wall to make things easier for him. She sat there for a while when he was safely up, warm and content in the sun, both listening and watching and meditating. When he acknowledged with his customary dignity his friends among the passers-by below, she stood up, her head on a level with his, and rejoiced with them. Then they went back into the house and there Mrs Tremorne ripped down the blackout curtains from her bedroom window, hung out a Union Jack, and tied a red, white and blue ribbon in a bow on Bel Ria's collar.

But in truth she herself seemed rejuvenated in this her eightieth year, for so much had happened, there was so much to look forward to, so many preparations afoot. Janet and Neil had their own quarters upstairs now, and it would not be long before he was demobbed. Her relief that the war was at last over was measured more by the fact that she no longer felt bound to supply His Majesty's Navy with knitted comforts, but could ply her needles instead in an endless stream of matinée jackets, bootees and bonnets for the child that was on the way. And the assurance that she would be the child's godmother and proxy grandmother all rolled into one gave her carte blanche to order the best in nursery furniture and equipment in the same manner as she had years before ordered the best for a nameless little dog.

There was another more immediate excitement to be realised too, the long awaited visit from Donald Sinclair. She could think of little else the week before. Bel Ria was shampooed, trimmed, combed and brushed to silken perfection, and she thought that he must sense something unusually exciting in the wind, for he became very restless and questioning the day before the visit.

She was alone in the house that day, a day that had become unexpectedly even more momentous: early in the morning Neil had taken Janet to the hospital – some three weeks earlier than had been anticipated. She hovered between the kitchen and the hall window, the crossword unsolved, her knitting untouched, unable to settle to anything.

The charged atmosphere in the house since that dawn awakening had affected Bel Ria too. He became increasingly restless as the morning wore on, panting, importuning, roaming from room to room, up and down the stairs, then back to her. He whined at the door to be let out, then minutes later scratched at it to be let in. She watched him settle on the sanctuary of the wall in the early afternoon almost with relief.

He was there when his soldier came walking up the road, searching for the house. Minutes before he came into view, Bel Ria half rose, ears pricked, tensed and ready. For the first time he jumped down off the wall on to the road. He waited, crouched low and quivering.

Donald Sinclair did not recognise him at first glance, so neatly unobtrusive against a peaceful suburban background; then, as he drew nearer, the unmistakable riveting eyes drew him back down the years to that road in France and the dusty desolate little figure with its rider clinging tightly around its neck. Then the eyes had been filled with wary entreaty; now they were bright and somehow calmly expectant. He waited there steadily, until that soldier who had once tried to drive him off, picked him up silently now and held him close in his arms. He buried his head in the man's jacket, as though seeking once more the reassurance of a bandage torn from familiar clothing.

Sinclair could feel the heart beating fast beneath his hands. He opened the gate and stood within for a long minute, for he was deeply moved, then he walked slowly towards the house.

Alice Tremorne came to the door, her face ashen; she had seen him coming from the window and thought he carried a dead or injured Bel. Wordlessly, she put out her hands to take him, but he resisted, burrowing his head back within the man's jacket. In a sudden flood of relief she realised who this stranger must be.

'I'm sorry, I must have given you a fright. I'm Donald Sinclair,' he said, and put Bel Ria down to steady her.

Her knees felt as though they were buckling. She tottered into the kitchen on his arm and sank into the nearest chair.

'How silly of me,' she said at last, the colour returning to her face. 'It has been such an eventful day—'

He brought her a glass of water. 'I think this is an occasion that calls for something a little stronger,' she said, managing a smile at last, and directed him to the cupboard with the Sloe Gin, '36.

'My best vintage,' she said as she poured two glasses. 'I never drink it without thinking of Bel – Bel Ria, I mean, he saved my life, you know, he found me—'

She broke off and looked across to where he sat now with his muzzle laid on the man's knee, whining softly. She had never seen him like this before, so tense that he was almost rigid, his whole being concentrated on the man, excluding her even when she had spoken his name.

'There is no need to ask if he recognised you,' she said, smiling, for strangely the exclusion did not rankle. She had warmed immediately to this tall gentle-faced man with the same soft accent as Neil, the same dark almost navy blue eyes. 'Oh, there is so much to tell you, so much to ask – let's begin at the beginning and go on to the end.'

The sloe gin reminded Donald Sinclair in its potency of the old man's fire-coursing brew. It might not be the beginning, but he spoke of this now, of the last sip taken on French soil with the young Fusilier, of the *Lancastria*'s last hours, and the long ordeal in the water when he had seen himself reflected in those same dark eyes that watched him now. And from there he went back to the first encounter with the caravan.

He was a natural story-teller. Sometimes the words came out as though he were half-speaking to himself, his face clearing as some long forgotten detail sprang to mind again, at other times frowning in concentration. Drawn on by Mrs Tremorne's rapt attention, her head nodding from time to time as some small blank was filled in for her, he recreated in vivid living detail the close security and love, the responsibility, the excitement, the tragedy and courage of those eventful missing hours in Bel Ria's life that he had shared.

She spoke only once, when he described the perfection of communication between the dark woman and her dog in the performance on the road.

'So that was what he was trying to tell me,' she said sadly, 'Oh, Bel, if only I had known—'

But Bel Ria had ears only for the inflections of this voice that stirred memory, this man who was his last link in the human chain that reached back to the rolling open roads of the caravan world, the chain that held him fast for so long.

It was almost dusk when the story ended. The kitchen was

very still and peaceful. Mrs Tremorne roused herself back to reality after a long silence. 'I wonder what his real name was,' she mused and she told of John Peel's hounds and how Bel had picked out his name.

'I don't think I heard her speak directly to him once,' said Donald Sinclair. 'She would nod, or use her hands, or just look his way and that was all. But it is curious that he picked on an English word like "bell".' He drew out of his pocket a white pillbox and handed it over. 'It was around his neck,' he explained, 'I brought it for good luck – for the bairn that's coming.'

Mrs Tremorne opened the box and took out a tiny silver bell, the handle threaded by a narrow metallic strip. She shook it gently, smiling at the unexpectedly clear sweet tone.

Bel Ria's head turned as though electrified by the sound, his ears pricked, then for the first time since Sinclair's arrival he came to her. His tail moved faster and faster, he cocked his head from one side to the other as she tinkled the bell again. She slipped the ribbon around his neck. He tossed his head, shook it, then moved it from side to side in a deliberate rhythmic control that kept the clapper chiming continuously. Enchanted, Mrs Tremorne clapped her hands in time.

'He had bells around his paws too when he danced on the road,' said Sinclair. He clicked his fingers and Bel Ria came running to sit before him, transformed with a jaunty confident excitement.

He offered his forepaws, one at a time with a demanding insistence. Donald Sinclair took each one in turn, encircling it with his fingers, smiling down regretfully, but Bel Ria seemed satisfied with the action. He stood stockstill between them for a moment, then with head erect, he straightened his back and extended his forepaws in the ritual that had always preceded the tantalising fragment of the dance bestowed from time to time on Mrs Tremorne.

He took the opening step – and at the very same moment there was a crashing bang as the front door slammed, footsteps ran across the hall, then the kitchen door burst open before Neil MacLean.

'Janet's fine!' he shouted, 'and it's a boy – Janet's got a fine wee boy for us!'

He rushed at Mrs Tremorne and hugged her, so carried away that he almost lifted her off her feet. Then he turned to Donald Sinclair and an incomprehensible flood of Gaelic goodwill followed, accompanied by much handshaking and backslapping.

Bel Ria was caught up in the excitement too. His years fell away and he raced around the kitchen, scattering the rugs on the linoleum. He skidded to a halt and barked before the group, but such was the jubilation that no one heard this rarest demand for notice. In an attempt to be more closely involved he jumped up on to a nearby chair, but abandoned it when Mrs Tremorne unknowingly dropped her fur wrap over his head when she went to find the hoarded whisky to wet the new Scot's head. His exuberance died away and he sat panting quietly by the door, the wrap still trailing from one shoulder.

They sat around the table after the initial toast of health, wealth and happiness to the new life. They grew ever more close and mellow as reminiscences and plans flowed back and forth. They drank a toast to Janet, and to one another.

'And to Bel Ria,' remembered Mrs Tremorne at last, looking down at him, remorseful at her oversight. 'To my darling Bel – for if it were not for you, the three of us would not be celebrating now.'

'To Bel—'

'And Ria—'

'And Bel Ria—' they said, and raised their glasses to him.

After the first commotion of congratulations had died down, he had crept back to sit by Sinclair, pressed close against his leg. Occasionally he had shaken his head in a bid for inclusion, but the small sweet sound of the bell went unheard below the cheerful voices. Then he had tried circling the group, pausing, concentrating intently on the faces as though willing them to glance down. He was patted absently by each in turn, but still the voices rose and fell, denying him. He whined, patently distressed and bewildered, as though he understood no meaning or intent from their intonations. Panting, he went to and from his waterbowl until it was empty, then returned to sit by the soldier.

'Bel – Ria – Bel Ria –' he heard at last, and the hand that lay on his neck threaded fingers through the ribbon there to set the bell tinkling clearly in the sudden silence.

It was his moment. He had the full spotlight of his audience's attention at last. He shook his head to set the bell ringing, rose, then straight and steady, his eyes fixed ahead, he pirouetted before them.

Mrs Tremorne had been privileged to see these opening movements of his inexplicable little dance. Neil MacLean had never seen or even known about it. Long ago, Donald Sinclair had been one of a spellbound audience that had watched it to the conclusion. But now in the gathering dusk of a silent room, the little dog did not dance for him, or for her, nor did he even look apprehensively in Neil MacLean's direction. He danced as though he must, for the one who taught him. But her bidding never came, there were no signalling fingers or tapping foot, no guiding flute to accompany him, and he became halting and uncertain in his steps. Panting hard now, shaking his head for the reassurance of the bell, he circled slowly and faltered, half-lowering himself to the floor, his head turning back as though in search.

Helpless and deeply disturbed, his audience watched. He rose again unsteadily, repeated the circle, and tried to follow on into a tight spin.

'Oh, no – *no*, Bel,' pleaded one; 'Let him be,' said another; and the third who alone could set this tragic pas de seul against its proper background, who alone understood its choreography, looked on silently.

But suddenly Bel Ria seemed to receive confidence. His

head went back and his eyes looked forward with a steady eagerness, as though long custom had recalled the closing movements and there was no longer any need for direction.

There was nothing to disquiet now in the certain dignity and perfection of his finale. He circled, slower and slower, his forepaws lowering and his head drooping to the proper spaced intervals, once more the perfectly controlled clockwork toy running down. But this time when he sank to the ground he did not rise again to take his applause and finish his act. It was already over.